PRETEND I'M YOURS

A Fake Marriage Romance

ELLA MILES

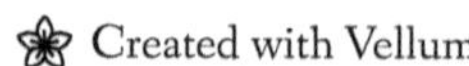 Created with Vellum

1 LARKYN

"I CAN'T DO THIS," I say, as Serena and I walk toward the front door of Sebastian's party.

Serena cuts her eyes to me. "You can totally do this."

I'm a twenty-two-year-old virgin. Tonight that changes.

I spent all afternoon scrolling through the ridiculously small number of men on my phone. Danny, Alan, Gavin, and Pat. None of them are great options to accomplish the deed. Danny is too short. Alan is too nice, and I think has a girlfriend. Gavin is hung up on Serena, and I don't want to sleep with him so that he can make Serena jealous. And Pat is not an option for so many reasons. But I need to find someone. Hence, why I'm attempting to get into the most exclusive party of the year. To find Mr. Perfect. I will not graduate from college next month still a virgin.

Who am I kidding? I once thought it mattered who the guy was. I wanted the ideal guy, to be in love. I wanted flowers and a sunset, followed by wine, candles, and a man who adored me and wanted my first time to be special. After four years of dating and no guy coming close to the picture I painted in my head, I'm desperate.

I want sex.

Maybe my first time won't be fantastic, but then I can experience a second or third time. And eventually, I'll meet a guy to give me the toe-curling moment I only dream about now.

I stumble again in my heels, and Serena takes my hand and rests it on her arm. "Well, you can as long as you don't fall flat on your face first." She chuckles. "Although, if you fell and showed the bouncer you aren't wearing any underwear, we wouldn't have any trouble getting in either. So, it doesn't matter what you do."

I glare at her. "Well, that wouldn't work because I'm wearing underwear. And I would like the school to not think of me as a laughing stock."

"Who cares if they do? We graduate in less than a month, and you won't have to see any of these people ever again."

I take a deep breath, letting the air fill my lungs before slowly exhaling. Serena's right. I can do this.

We strut, arm in arm, up the long driveway to the door. We get behind a group of loud girls chatting excitedly. I recognize them. They are in a sorority, and no doubt were invited. They are all in short, expensive dresses that accentuate their bodies and show how much money they are from. They don't flirt their way in. They are invited in.

We are next, and my stomach is doing flips. My legs are shaky, and not just because of the heels my feet aren't used to being shoved in. My heart is fluttering a million miles a minute in my chest. I should have taken a shot with Serena before we came.

"Name?" the tall man asks.

"Serena Toomer and Larkyn Day."

He scans his list, not bothering to glance at us. Our plan isn't going to work.

"Your names aren't listed," he says.

"Let's go," I whisper to Serena.

She ignores me, looking past the bouncer, who won't be seduced since he won't stop staring at his clipboard.

"Sebastian!" she shouts.

My eyes widen in fear. "What are you doing?" I hiss.

"Getting you in so you can get laid."

Sebastian turns in our direction and grins at us goofily. He doesn't know either of us, but Serena smiles at him and his eyes drag over my low-cut dress, and suddenly he's walking our way.

"Hey!" Sebastian says, and my heart sinks. I bite my bottom lip to keep from drooling. He's hot in his dark jeans and buttoned down shirt, which is open at the top, revealing his muscular chest. All he said was 'hey,' and my body reacts like he said the most charming pickup line. I need to get laid, so I stop fawning over every guy like this.

"Hey, we aren't on the list. A mixup, I'm sure. Any possibility you can change that?" Serena asks, shoving me forward, so my body brushes against his.

I'm going to kill her for this later.

But it does the trick. Sebastian's eyes glue to the cleavage the dress makes me appear to have, and then down to my abs, defined beneath the material.

"Absolutely!" Sebastian holds out his arm to me, and I nervously take it. I cut my eyes to Serena who winks at me as Sebastian leads me into his house.

"I'm sorry you weren't on the list. I don't know how I missed a beautiful woman like you. I wish we had classes together so I could have noticed you earlier."

I bite my lip and blush. "We do take a class together.

You are in my marketing class." I don't add we did a group project together last year in finance, and he has been in almost every single one of my classes starting freshman year since we are both on the same business track.

He doesn't blush or show signs of embarrassment. I wish he would have noticed me before or realize who I am. I know his name and who he is.

"What's your name?" he asks.

"Larkyn Day."

He grins. "I love that name. I'm Sebastian King."

His smoldering blue eyes look at me, and my heart is his. I don't know how I ended on the arm of Sebastian, basically the king of the popular crowd, and I know that soon, he'll be leaving me alone to enjoy his other guests, but I'll remember this moment forever.

"Can I get you a drink?" he asks.

I nod, knowing this is when he dismisses me. I look hot, but I'm not hot enough. I'm wearing a nude colored sparkly dress, but it's not slutty enough to compare with the women skirting around us in dresses that are so short they can't wear underwear. Their dresses leave no curve on their bodies to the imagination. While I, I just hope this dress is enough to snag one decent looking guy that isn't already too drunk to fuck me.

Sebastian leads me over to one of the bars and gets me a white wine without asking what I want. He gets himself a beer. I start peering around for where Serena is so she can help me find a guy for the night.

I feel a hand on my waist and glance down to see Sebastian's hand wrapped around my waist, pulling me closer to him.

"Do you have a date for tonight?" he asks, leaning down to my ear so he can talk to me over the loud music blasting through the house. The band is out back, and we are in the front of the house so I can only imagine how loud it is out back.

"No," I say, taking a sip of my wine, so I have something to do with my hands, and I can stop blushing. The wine tastes overly sweet. I don't often drink, caring too much about staying healthy, but when I do, I rarely choose wine.

"Good, I needed someone to hang out with tonight."

Yep, now I'm blushing again like an idiot. I need to stop getting so affected by this man. I've had a crush on him since forever, but that doesn't mean anything. He's just being nice. He won't be the guy that pops my cherry. Even though I should be searching for that guy, I can't pass up an opportunity to spend some time with Sebastian first.

"You don't have a date either?" I ask, finally getting my voice back.

He looks down at me, his eyes lingering on my cleavage. "Now, I do."

My heart stops. Sebastian did not just say that. I must have misheard him. He's the most popular guy at our school. He can date any woman he wants. He's fucked most of the popular women. He doesn't want me to be his date.

But the way his hand grips my waist, as he starts leading me outside, it seems I heard him right.

Eyes. That's all I see when we walk outside, where the band is playing by the infinity pool. Everyone's eyes are on me. The guy's eyes rake over my cleavage and smirk at Sebastian approvingly. While the women alternate being glaring at me and giving Sebastian a sweet, come-here look.

I swallow, trying to get the lump in my throat to go down, but it's no use. I'm not in my element. I don't do parties. I don't hang out in crowds. I don't like attention. I prefer running down the road by myself with nothing but my playlist to keep me company.

Sebastian ignores the stares and leads me over to where a group of his friends is hanging out drinking their beer and wine around a cocktail table.

He greets them, but never takes his hand off my waist.

"And you are?" one of the women to my right asks. Her voice is much too high. And she chugs her wine in one motion, before she looks at me again, as she makes a noise in her throat that sounds like a threatening growl.

"I'm—"

"This is Larkyn. She's my date for tonight," Sebastian says, pulling me tighter into his body, so I get a whiff of his cologne. It's a strong scent, and it seems he used too much, but it doesn't matter. He's still appealing no matter how much of the stuff he uses. Especially, when he keeps calling me his date.

The woman scuffs and signals the waiter for another drink. The three men standing around the table all chuckle in unison like they know a secret I'm not in on.

Sebastian glances behind us. "Dance with me."

"Um..." I don't get a chance to say I don't dance. That I've *never* danced. He takes the last swig of his beer before taking my almost full glass of wine from my hands and sets it down on the cocktail table.

His hand moves to the small of my back as he leads me to the dance floor. My body feels hot as I gaze around at all the other people on the floor grinding their bodies together. It doesn't look like dancing. It looks like sex.

My eyes stare up at Sebastian's as he stands in front of me and starts moving to the music. While I stand frozen. I don't know how to dance to this music. He doesn't seem to notice. Instead, he grabs my hand and gently pulls me to his body. He twirls me around and grabs my hips, pulling me to his body, so my back presses against his front.

His hands guide me, as his body sways to the music, and I do the same. Our bodies glide together to the beat of the music. I don't know what to do with my hands, but I find them running over his, which glue to my hips.

I spot Serena out of the corner of my eye. She's dancing with her boyfriend. She must have snuck him in.

I smile.

Tonight is going to be a good night, even if nothing else happens. Dancing in Sebastian's arms, I can pretend I'm his. Pretend I live in a world of popular kids with fancy cars. I can pretend this is what I want. And who I am.

"You smell incredible," Sebastian says, grinding harder until I can feel the strain of his erection against my ass.

I blush. I can't take a compliment.

I want to turn and look at him, but I don't dare. My knees are already weak enough. If I turn and see his blue eyes staring at me like he wants to devour me, I'll lose my mind. I'd probably melt right here. Merely disappear into a puddle on the floor. Or worse yet, he might kiss me, and I'm afraid the act of him sweeping his tongue into my mouth might be enough for my body to orgasm. Here, in front of everyone.

He needs to stop the public displays of affection before I lose it.

He doesn't listen to my inner turmoil though. Instead, he makes it worse, by nuzzling my neck. And then, yep, I'm going to lose it, he kisses my neck, running his slick tongue across my sensitive skin.

My knees buckle, and he catches me in his arms, tightening his grip around my waist.

He chuckles. "Don't worry; I got you. I'm used to women getting a little weak around me."

My cheeks are bright red now. He's cocky, but I don't care. Usually, I would hate guys who say shit like that. But not guys who are as hot as Sebastian is. Not when he's holding me tightly against his hard body. I'm especially intrigued by the hardness, which continues to push roughly into my ass. Every time I move, it grows larger until I'm terrified, but also desperate, to feel the slick beast inside me.

Sebastian King could be my first. And that petrifies me. He could ruin me for all other men. Because it's not like he will stick around after the first night. Not when he realizes how inexperienced I am in bed.

He starts kissing my neck again, and my eyes close, enjoying his touch and trying to forget about everything else. Who cares that this won't last? I didn't set out tonight to get into a relationship. I set out to find a guy who wants to fuck me. And Sebastian King wants to fuck me.

"Want to get another drink?" he says suddenly against my neck.

I moan.

He chuckles again.

Shit, I need to stop moaning and getting weak in the knees every time he speaks, or he's going to realize I've never had a man touch me like he's groping me now.

"Drink?" he asks again, reminding me of the question.

Drink? He wants to get a drink now?

I sigh. I guess Sebastian isn't as into dancing as I am with him. Drinking means he won't have his hands all over my body as he does now. But I don't have a choice. If I say no, he might stop hanging out with me altogether.

"Sure."

I open my eyes as his hand slides down to my ass. I squeak when he pinches it, and I chance a glance.

He's smirking at me, his hands guiding me off the dance floor back to where his friends are still drinking. I glance over at them as we approach with his hand still on my ass. They are all staring, and then the woman who asked who I was before is no longer blinking her eyelashes as she glares, trying to make me disappear with her eyes.

I swallow hard and turn my glance away from them, trying to keep my confidence to continue letting Sebastian touch me like he is.

My eyes lock with a pair of dark eyes. The eyes of a man sitting by himself. He's holding a full whiskey glass, wearing a dark suit, which makes him blend in with the darkness around him. I can't get a good look at his features, except for his eyes. Intensely would be an understatement. This man has already undressed me with his eyes, peeled off a few layers of skin, and reached my soul.

I don't know who he is or why he's staring. He glances away a second later, and I'm not even sure if he was staring at me.

I turn my attention back to the table as we stop at the edge of it.

A waiter appears the second she sees Sebastian off the dance floor and without a drink.

"Wine again or something stronger?" he asks me.

My stomach churns and my heart races.

"Stronger."

He grins, liking my answer. He speaks to the waiter, but I don't hear what he says, and a few minutes later I've taken three shots of tequila. I feel good. Amazing. And I no longer give a shit what Avril and Naomi think of me. That's what the bitches' names are, I've learned.

I've also learned drinking with Sebastian is just as enjoyable as dancing. He's spent the entire time with his arms wrapped around my body while he presses against me from behind. The only time he ever stops is when he has to speak with the waiter to get us another round of drinks.

"Hell yes!" Blake says. This is the third time I've heard him say, 'hell yes' to anything anyone suggests, so it's not surprising he says it now.

"Fuck yea. It's finally warm enough to use the pool without you women complaining it's cold," Duncan says, eyeing Naomi.

Naomi doesn't look at Duncan's hungry eyes. She's only interested in Sebastian's. I try not to let any jealousy in. But I know Naomi and Sebastian have hooked up before. And if I don't hold Sebastian's attention, he could easily decide Naomi is the better option for tonight.

Sebastian holds a shot of tequila out to me, and I grab the glass, although I'm not sure if my stomach can handle another.

I suck in a sharp breath when I feel him place the salt on my neck. I've seen several of the men do it to some of the other girls here before. But he's never done it to me.

I feel lightheaded, like I'm floating out of my body. Even though he's had his mouth on my neck several times now, this feels more intimate.

"Shots!" Duncan yells.

Then, Sebastian's mouth is on my neck, sucking, as he licks the salt off, and then we both do the shot. I shake my head, hating the taste since I forgot the salt first. I need to try this game in reverse, so I get to lick the salt of one of his body parts. But I'm not brazen enough to try it, not without his suggestion.

He grabs for a lime and expertly drops it, so it buries in

my cleavage. I go to snatch it, but he spins me around and leans down, retrieving it with his teeth as his lips brush over my cleavage.

My body warms, and my thoughts shatter. That was...hot.

He sucks on the lime a minute and removes it, smirking at me as usual.

I'm frozen. I can't move. I'm pretty sure I just dreamed that, because there is no way Sebastian had his face buried between my breasts.

But I get an evil glare again from Naomi, and I know it happened.

Sebastian interlocks his hand with mine, and he tugs me toward the pool, which has been mostly empty the entire night, except for the occasional drunk guy who decides to toss a girl into the pool fully clothed. *Why do guys think that's a good idea?* Women *hate* it. There is no way they are persuading any woman to sleep with them after that.

I glance around, looking for the pool house or some-place where people are changing clothes. I don't see one, but this house is large enough I'm sure there is one.

My eyes pop open when I see Naomi grab the hem of her dress and jerk it over her head until she's left in nothing but her black lacy thong underwear. Her dress was low cut, so she isn't wearing a bra, and she has no problem with the stares she's getting. I'm pretty sure every man in the area's erection grew at the sight of her.

Shit.

I can't strip. I'm not wearing a bra either, and there is no way any guy here is going to be impressed by my much smaller chest.

Women all around me continue stripping down to their

bras and underwear, while the men remove their dress pants and jackets down to their underwear.

"Oh!" I squeal unexpectedly, when one of the guys strips until he's butt naked.

Sebastian laughs.

"Don't worry. I won't let Duncan touch you or come near you. You're mine, for tonight," Sebastian says.

I grin like an idiot. I love hearing him call me *his*.

But my grin falters the second I see Sebastian begin to strip next to me. His shirt is gone, revealing the muscles I've been feeling all night, and then his pants are gone, making his erection much more noticeable beneath his boxer briefs.

I gulp as my eyes rake over his body and become glued to his straining cock. I need to stop staring, but I can't. I want to know what that glorious erection would feel like rocking in my body. But it also terrifies me because I'm not sure my body is ready for such a massive intrusion.

"Like what you see?" he chuckles in my ear.

I force my eyes to drag up to his eyes instead of his cock. But my heart hates me a little for it.

"Sorry."

He lifts my chin up and then his lips are on mine. Exploring, tasting, devouring.

He stops and kisses me a moment later. "Don't be sorry," he says like the kiss was nothing.

Kisses mean nothing to a guy like Sebastian, but to me, kisses like that are rare. No, kisses like that never happen in my world.

I'm frozen as I watch Sebastian walk to the pool's diving board.

"Come on, baby," he says, doing a flip before diving in, in a perfect arch. His body gracefully hits the water and people cheer, holding up their hands, giving him a score of a ten for his incredible dive.

My mouth drops open, and I know I'm drooling. I snap my mouth shut, but it doesn't stop my erratic breathing.

I start taking a step forward, needing to be in Sebastian's arms. I realize I'm supposed to strip, so I hesitate at the edge of the pool while a dozen or so eyes stare up at me.

My hands tremble. I can't do this. I can't strip in front of these people. I'm not ashamed of my body, in fact, I love my body. But these people come from money. They have perfect bodies to go with their flashy dresses and expensive houses. Their parents have provided them with an incredible start to life with substantial trust funds waiting for them when they graduate to turn into billion-dollar businesses.

They are elite, while I'm ordinary. I may have abs of steel, but I don't come from money. I didn't get a boob-job like half the women in the pool to add curves. I'm flat, yet strong. And I have no intention of showing them just how ordinary I am.

Sebastian stares up at me expectedly, but even his gorgeous body isn't enough to convince me to strip naked.

Then, I see Naomi swimming toward him planning on taking advantage of my hesitation. If I don't jump in, she'll be the one in Sebastian's bed tonight. Not me.

My hand goes to my back, pulling on the zipper without thinking. The zipper slides halfway down and then stops. No matter how hard I pull the zipper, it won't budge.

Naomi swims faster, and I jerk my body, trying to get the damn zipper to go down far enough that I can rip the dress over my head. The jerking makes me lose my balance though, and before I realize what's happening, I feel the warm water consuming me as I crash into the pool.

I pop my head back up hoping people won't care, but of

course, they care. Laughter, hysterical laughter is breaking out all around me. Even Sebastian is laughing at me.

Dammit.

I give up. I can't fit in with these people even for one night. Not long enough to get laid, that's for sure. I should have stuck with someone in my own league.

Sebastian swims toward me.

"Here, let me help you," he says.

"No, that's ok—"

I stop when his hands touch my back. In the few moments of embarrassment, I forgot how electrifying it feels to have his hands on my skin.

He unzips the dress and reaches for the hem, pulling the dress off my wet body. No one can see my body under the water. This might actually work out for me. Then I move and realize my stupid heels are still on.

Before I realize what's happening, Sebastian has lifted me to the edge of the pool so that he can work on removing my shoes.

Silence.

I glance around, as the stares burn into my body. No one is laughing. And the men are wide-eyed as they stare at my body. My cheeks flush and my heart races, but I soon realize they are looking at me like they ogled at Naomi. Even some of the women are gazing at me appreciatively.

"Wow," Sebastian says, as he removes my second shoe. Somehow he already removed the first one without me noticing.

My eyes fall to his, as he stares at my boobs, and then my abs, like I did his cock earlier.

"Like what you see?" I ask, boldly repeating his words.

He smirks and grabs my waist, pulling me back into the pool and to his body.

"Fuck yea. Incredible."

I smile.

"How did you get abs like this?" he asks, raking his fingers over my stomach. "I might need some tips." He winks.

I laugh. "I don't think you need help getting abs." I glance down at his eight-pack.

He shrugs. "I guess we have something in common."

He kisses my lips again without warning, while my legs wrap around his waist and my arms wrap around his neck. I've never been this naked with a man before. But I'm not sure I want to wear clothes ever again.

His kisses trail down my neck, and I shiver.

"You cold?" he asks.

I shake my head no, as I shudder again when he licks my neck.

He smirks. "We are getting out. Larkyn's cold."

I pout. "I'm not—"

His lips slam into mine again, shutting me up. I moan as his tongue brushes against mine. I kiss him back hungrily, knowing at least my kissing skills are on par. But if he wants sex or a blow job, he's going to have to take the lead, because I have no clue what I'm doing.

He finally forces me to stop kissing when I realize the others are protesting us leaving the pool.

"I'm sorry, but Larkyn's cold. I'm going to get her some clothes from upstairs to change into. You guys enjoy the pool. We will see you later." He winks at me to play along with being cold.

"Yes, I'm so cold," I say, faking trembling again to keep up the ruse.

Sebastian chuckles as he carries me up the steps of the pool. I keep my legs wrapped around his waist, and my front pressed firmly against his chest, so no one gets a view of my breasts again.

"Let's get you into some dry clothes, but first you need to get naked and have a hot shower to warm you up."

I bite my lip to keep from smiling too brightly because I know what he's not saying. He wants to fuck me. And I'm more than happy to let him.

SEBASTIAN PUSHES the door open to his bedroom and kicks it shut behind him.

"Should you lock that?" I ask, between kisses, but I realize I don't care if the door is locked or not. If locking the door means having to stop kissing for a second, then I prefer unlocked.

He doesn't answer me. He kisses me until I'm moaning and purring like a kitten without an off switch.

He pushes me back against the bed, as his rocklike body stays cemented to mine, our smooth wet skin slick against each other.

"Fuck, why didn't I find you earlier?" he growls, as he leans back to earn a view of my body again.

My instinct is to cover my body, but then I notice the way his nostrils flare every time he takes a breath. The way his lips part a little more and his breathing is erratic with every gaze of my body. He wants my body. Just as I want his.

His fingers move down my body and hook into my white cotton panties. Most women wear lace thongs or nothing at all. I didn't want to lose my virginity while feeling like someone else. But now, in this moment, I wish I'd borrowed something of Serena's as she offered. At least I shaved.

My heart pounds in my chest as his fingers start lowering my panties. Fluttering creeps up from deep in my belly. And an unfamiliar ache throbs between my legs, begging for relief.

This is it. I'm going to be completely naked in front of a man. And he's going to fuck me.

This is my last chance to back out. His eyes stare at mine, give me one final warning to back out now, because once he starts, there is no stopping him. But I don't want him to stop.

My friends told me their first times were horrible. The guy was inexperienced and didn't know what he was doing. But my first time is going to be incredible. Because I'm doing it with Sebastian fucking King. The king of experience, and the epitome of sexiness.

I swallow, trying to find my voice to tell him this is precisely what I want. But swallowing doesn't do enough to give me a voice. I have none. Sebastian stole it. It's his now, like every other part of my body. I hope I can retrieve it when he's done with me. Because otherwise, this is going to hurt like a motherfucker when he leaves.

He leers like he knows exactly what he's doing. Ruining me. Making my body experience things I didn't think I could feel for a man I just met. Then shred my heart.

It's still worth it.

He starts lowering my panties, and my hips buck, impatiently needing him to move faster. Not because I'm afraid one of us will back out, but because my body literally can't handle another second of being a virgin. I need his cock inside me, the ache between my legs is building, and I can't hold it off any longer.

I need him rocking back and forth in an exquisite way, making me scream his name and want him forever. I'm not stupid; I know I only get him for tonight. My name doesn't have enough pull in this town for him to want me for more than one night. And I'm not experienced enough to make sex worth him coming back for more.

"You need to get your ass back downstairs now. Duncan got in a fight with James over Naomi," a beaming voice makes me jump.

Sebastian curses under his breath, but doesn't move as he frowns, straddling my body on the bed, like he's going to regret his next move.

I can't see who entered Sebastian's bedroom, Sebastian's body is still covering me. Which means the intruder can't see my naked body either. It should bring me some comfort, but it doesn't.

"Go to hell Kade! Can't you tell I'm busy?" Sebastian says.

Kade? I try to figure out where I know that name, but I can't place it. It's familiar, but isn't. I don't think I've had any classes with a Kade, and I don't think Sebastian has any close friends named Kade. I don't know what the hell he is doing here.

"I don't give a shit. I'm not here to clean up your messes."

Sebastian rolls his eyes and turns his head abruptly toward the intruder as his still hard cock presses deeper between my legs. So close, yet so far.

"Then, why are you here? I thought you were here to look out for your little brother and to celebrate me graduating next month. I thought you grew a heart and gave a shit about me?"

Kade growls. "I am here for you. You're an adult now, though. I'm not dealing with this shit anymore. You do what you want, just thought you should know Duncan and James are fighting. Last I checked, they broke two bar stools and were getting close to the big screen TV of yours. And I'm pretty sure Mrs. Plitt called the cops."

"Shit," Sebastian curses, as his body springs off of me and races out of the room.

I don't rank as high as his TV. My eyes water, but I blink once, and the threat of tears is gone. I won't cry over a guy. No way. That won't happen. *Ever.*

I shiver, my body cold now Sebastian's warm body is no longer pressed against me. Suddenly, I'm acutely aware I'm naked except for my panties. And Kade still hasn't left.

My hand reaches out instinctively for the blanket lying on the edge of the bed. I need to cover my mostly naked body as fast as possible. Before I yell at this asshole for ruining my night.

Maybe if I stay here naked in Sebastian's bed, he will find me when he returns and pick up right where he left off?

Who am I kidding? I have the worst luck when it comes to guys. This isn't the first time I've tried to lose my virginity. I've had guys throw up on me, fall asleep, or get a text from an ex all seconds before we were about to fuck. This is just my luck. The universe really doesn't want me to have sex.

I jerk the blanket to my body, attempting to cover myself, as I get the nerve to glance up at the man standing over me.

He's gaping at me. His eyes take their time as he lazily explores my body with his, like my body is his to peer at.

My body warms under his gaze, and I forget why I wanted to cover up with the blanket in the first place. He's a complete stranger to me, but I let him stare at my body that is barely covered with a blanket. I want him to gape. Need him to.

It's a different stare than how Sebastian looked at me. But then, this man looks nothing like Sebastian. Sebastian has light shady hair and a fit body with a little stubble on his chin. This man is much taller than Sebastian. His hair is dark, and there is stubble on his chin and neck, although from the business suit he is wearing, I'm sure he shaved this morning, but it grew back by the end of the day.

Sebastian is still a boy. A college guy who lives for fun. Kade is a man. I'm not sure he even knows what fun is from how he's standing, like something serious is happening.

I thought I wanted Sebastian, but maybe Kade would do. He might not be as light-hearted as Sebastian is, but he oozes maturity. Kade knows how to handle a woman in bed, and the glimmer in his eyes says he would be happy to help me out.

I stare a moment longer, realizing the familiarity in his gaze. He was the pair of dark eyes I saw staring at me earlier. But his eyes aren't dark, not now that I've looked at them closer. They are auburn. Brightly glowing as he continues staring.

"You're staring," I say, pointing out the obvious. My voice is snarky, but I don't cover up or tell him to get the fuck out. Because I'd gladly swap one brother for the other.

What's wrong with me? I've become one of those women. The kind who only sees guys like a piece of meat, who are here to fuck me. The kind who doesn't require any standards. No date. No conversation. No romance. I'm *that* desperate for sex.

He grins, and I see the little dimple form on his rough cheek. Yep, I'm one of those women who will give up my body to a sex god without thinking about the consequences. I've become the women I hate, and I won't apologize for it. I may not be able to convince a man like this to date me or take me seriously. But right now, dripping wet and practically naked, I know I can get him to fuck me. No man can resist a naked woman.

Kade closes the door Sebastian left cracked open when he dashed out. I hear the sharp lock of the door as he turns the lock, preventing Sebastian or anyone from entering.

My eyes widen, and I bite my lip to keep from smiling too wide.

I'm going to taste two *King's* in one night. My luck has changed.

He turns, and his eyes sink into my body again, making me squirm.

I want him.

He wants me.

Regret can form in the morning, now all I feel is lust.

My eyes cut to the bulge in his pants, confirming what his eyes are telling me. He wants me. There is no doubt about it.

He walks toward me, but I can't keep my eyes off the damn bulge. My cheeks flush the longer I stare, but I don't think there is any way I can be more embarrassed than I've already been tonight.

His hands press on either side of my head, but I can't focus on anything except his face that hovers over mine. He's going to kiss me.

I wet my lips in anticipation. Not sure how Kade's lips will be able to top Sebastian's, but as his lips lower and my toes curl before he touches me, I think he might be able to kiss better.

My heart pounds, my breathing stops, and my eyes close waiting for the kiss.

No kiss happens.

My eyes fly open, and he's smirking over me.

"Get dressed Larkyn, and I'll call you a car."

My mouth falls open, and my eyes widen. *How does he know my name? And why does he want me to get dressed and leave?* I thought...*shit*. He's not into me at all. His night, with his own date, was probably interrupted to deal with Sebastian's problems. But I don't remember a women sitting next to him when he was staring.

"What?" That's what comes out of my mouth. I'm a genius.

Kade pulls away. And I'm cold. And pissed.

I jump out of the bed letting the blanket fall to the bed. I'm still naked except for my panties as I watch Kade dig through Sebastian's drawers.

My anger pulses through me, but I don't know what to do with it. I'm not confrontational. I can't even stand up for basic things I want in my life. I have no idea how to stand up to a complete stranger. But if I don't do something, my anger is going to explode out of me.

"You don't get to tell me what to do! Sebastian invited me up here. I'll wait for him to return." I cross my arms over my chest as I glare at him. *There.* I did it. I told someone what I was thinking when I was feeling it. Mission accomplished.

Except Kade either didn't hear me or is completely ignoring me as he pulls some clothes out of the drawer and slams it shut, making me jump.

He gradually turns to face me.

"You don't want to lose your virginity to an ass like Sebastian."

My cheeks turn a brighter shade of red. "How do you…" I can't finish the sentence. It's not like 'virgin' is etched across my chest. The only person who knows is Serena, and she wouldn't tell a soul. He doesn't know I'm a virgin. It's a guess to get me riled up.

"I'm not a vir—"

He laughs. "Yes, you are. Now, get dressed." He thrusts the clothes into my hands. I take them because I'm too shocked to think through any of my actions.

"I don't know what my brother was doing with someone like you," he says, under his breath.

But I hear his words. And they sting like hell. *Someone like me.* Of course, I'm not good enough for his brother. I don't have a name worthy of this town. I don't have a business waiting for me to be able to take over when I graduate. My parents didn't donate thousands of dollars to the school. I'm a nothing. A nobody. And apparently, I'm not even worthy to fuck Sebastian for one night.

I want to yell. I want to scream. Tell Kade he's wrong. That Sebastian doesn't deserve me. But I've lost my voice. I can't whisper, let alone scream.

I grab the white T-shirt and jerk it over my head as a pair of shorts falls to the floor. I march toward him, hoping I'm daring enough to speak when I'm right in his face. I open my mouth and nothing.

He raises an eyebrow and crosses his arms over his chest while he waits.

I hate his smug expression. I may not be able to find the words, but my anger has focused elsewhere.

I knee him hard in the balls and turn, unlock the door,

and storm out. I hear him groaning in pain as I exit, and now it's my turn to smirk.

A smirk that is wiped from my face as I hear his words, "Sebastian definitely shouldn't be with a woman like you. You're the kind who would get pregnant after one fuck, and he'd be yours forever."

Tears. Damn tears.

No.

If there is one thing I'm good at, it's *not* crying. Or caring. Or thinking about these foolish people. I don't need their approval. I'm happy with who I am. I don't want to be invited to their dumb parties. I don't want one of their elites to be my first, or my second, or third.

Kade did me a favor. I almost made a huge mistake giving Sebastian something so precious. He would have ruined me. And not in the 'now I have high expectations for sex' kind of way. He would have torn my heart to shreds when he made me realize he only fucked me because I looked hot for a moment in a dress, and I was his new infatuation. Or the more likely scenario, he was drunk and he'd already fucked all the women at his party.

I'll keep my virginity until I find a guy who thinks of me as somebody.

I storm down the stairs, and I feel everyone gawking.

Shit.

I'm only wearing a white T-shirt and my panties. I didn't think to pick up the shorts I dropped.

I hear the snickers. This should be the most embarrassing moment of the night. It's not. And I refuse to go back upstairs to put more clothes on. Not even to retrieve my dress and shoes I left upstairs. I refuse.

Instead, I keep walking through the crowd searching for

Serena, but I can't find her anywhere. I didn't bring my phone. There was nowhere to hide it in my dress, and I didn't want to keep up with a purse. So I can't call her or an Uber to take me home. Not that I could afford an Uber even if I had my phone.

I should have waited for Kade to call me a car before I kneed him in the balls.

I grin again, thinking about how he's going to spend the rest of his night with an ice pack to his crotch.

Worth it.

I step out into the chilly night, my arms wrapping around myself and my legs sprouting goosebumps. My feet tingle from the cold concrete. *When did it get so cold out? It's almost May. It's supposed to be warm.*

I look down the long driveway that leads to a dark street. I live four miles from here. It's nothing, and if I jogged, I'd be home in twenty minutes.

But I don't have any shoes on.

It's cold.

It's dark.

And I'm pissed and frustrated, when I should be satisfied and blissfully ignorant. I should be asleep upstairs in Sebastian's bed.

Instead, I'm walking home in the dark. *Fuck my life.*

3 KADE

WHAT THE HELL is wrong with me?

My dick is hard, and for once in my life, I didn't take advantage of a woman I desperately wanted. Her eyes were a fierce shade of blue, the curl in her shoulder length blonde hair hung loose, and her body, *damn*. Her abs alone had me drooling and wanting to fuck her without thinking about the consequences. Her muscles rippled through her body. I've never seen a more toned body on a woman. And I can only imagine the positions I could put her in.

But she is too young and inexperienced for me. And I don't do Sebastian's sloppy seconds. I shouldn't be hard.

But I am. Painstakingly *hard*. I'm cursing for wearing such tight pants. I consider taking them off and jacking off, before heading back down, but I don't have time.

She kneed me in the balls, and yea, that hurt like hell, but it's nothing compared to how my dick aches at not fucking her. Her body was screaming for me to fuck her. I should receive a medal for chivalry after this is all over. Sebastian would have fucked her and hurt her, I would have fucker her and demolished her.

I jog out of the room to chase after her but stop after only making it to the door. I bend over trying to deal with the agony. Twinging, throbbing pain that won't subside until I spend my night with an ice pack on my balls or by fucking a woman in my bed. I prefer the latter. At least if I'm fucking, my dick will stop suffering.

Stop being a wuss.

I force myself to start running again, and I jog down the stairs ignoring the torment, biting my lip, so I don't let out girlish screams bursting to be let out with every step I take. *Damn, Larkyn.*

The pounding in my head returns when I step foot back downstairs, the house full of beating music. *I'm too old for this shit,* I think. Most people are far too drunk at this point. Women are stripping, and I see more bras and exposed breasts than at a strip club. Men are taking advantage, pressing women up against walls, and trying to sneak them upstairs.

Ugh.

I like partying, but not like this. This is sloppy and gross. I much prefer to hang out in one of the bars I own. More control, and fewer teenagers.

I step over a mountain of broken glass. Sebastian should learn to serve these idiots with solo cups. Someone always cuts themselves on the broken glass inevitably covering the floor after a dozen people drop their glasses because they're too drunk to hold a fucking drink.

Sebastian thinks because he comes from money all his parties need to be fancy. Why can't he learn to have a college party without all the extravagance? It would suit these people better, no matter how they view themselves.

I search the main floor and peak out into the backyard,

but I don't find Larkyn. She left. Had a friend take her home or called an Uber. Either way, she's no longer my problem. I need to forget about her.

I spot Sebastian out of the corner of my eye doing shots on Naomi's stomach.

I rub the back of my neck as I stare at him. He's never going to grow up. At least he is playing with a woman who understands what's at stake. She's on an even playing field with Sebastian. Unlike Larkyn, who was clueless about what she was getting herself into.

The TV is still hanging on the wall. Sebastian made it down in time to save his precious TV. And then, just as easily, forgot all about Larkyn. *Idiot.*

Smooth hands dance over my chest and wrap tightly around my neck as a boa constrictor wraps around its prey.

I pretend I can't breathe, motioning with my hands to my neck that Harlow's hands are too tight.

She laughs but doesn't loosen her grip on my neck.

"You can't resist me, so don't pretend. I like playing this game we have going on between us, but don't pretend we don't both know how this is going to end. I'm going to be naked in your bed by the end of the night," Harlow says.

I frown. No way in hell is that happening. I fucked her once, months ago. And I knew the second my dick touched her pussy it was a mistake. The sex was good, if not forgettable. Normally, it would have been fine. I wouldn't regret having sex with a woman as hot as Harlow, but fucking Harlow broke my one rule. I don't fuck women from Santa Barbara.

Women here aren't like women in LA. Women in LA know I'm only good for one fuck, and then they need to move on to the next millionaire or billionaire. Here though, they become attached. They want more. Women here are bred to search for a man with a name they can pass to their children and continue the legacy. And I happen to have a very powerful name in this town.

"Not going to fucking happen, Harlow. We had our one time, I don't go back for a second round," my voice sounds harsh, but I have to be cruel. She won't get the message if I'm not.

I untangle myself from her tentacles, as I try to disappear into the crowd. I should have stayed hidden in the shadows. I could watch the show without being noticed. But my brother had to go and be a dumbass and I have to save him, and the poor girl he almost ruined, like always.

Harlow yells after me, but I keep moving, only stopping to grab a beer from one of the waiters. I need it if I'm going to survive the rest of the night. I'd rather have another whiskey, but I need to stay sober to keep Sebastian out of trouble. I need some alcohol to keep myself from going off on Harlow, though.

Fuck this night.

I shouldn't have come back here, even if it was necessary.

I think I've finally evaded Harlow when a new warm body presses up against mine.

I don't recognize the woman, but she reeks of alcohol and vomit. Not an endearing combination.

I grab her shoulders to move her out of my way. She stumbles as I move her, and I hold her shoulder longer than I want.

"Kade King, I can't believe you're here. I've had such a big crush on you."

"You should drink some water," I say, flagging down a waiter and grabbing a glass of water to hand the woman.

She grins.

Shit, I know that grin. This is what I get for being nice and trying to help a woman.

"I want to have your babies Kade King!" she says, screaming.

My lips pull back tightly. I'm never coming to one of Sebastian's ridiculous parties again. In fact, this might be the last time I visit this town.

"Drink the water," I say, glancing around for her date or a friend to pass her off to. A man is standing behind her, eyeing her. I don't know if he's her date or not, but she's his problem now. I give him a, 'take care of her, don't fuck her,' glare and push her into his arms.

He looks happy, yet terrified. I roll my eyes and storm away. *Welcome to my world.*

Why do women think I want a baby? I already have one dealing with Sebastian.

I finish my loop around after thoroughly losing Harlow. I stand in the corner of the living room where Sebastian does another shot off Naomi, this time from between her boobs.

I nurse my beer, trying to blend into the corner as I keep an eye on my brother. He's done fucking everything up for me. This is the last major party of the year before graduation. He needs to make it through tonight without doing any damage.

"We need to talk," Harlow says, her body standing firmly in front of me, her hands crossed over her chest, and her face is fierce, in a don't mess with me sort of way.

I sigh as I glance at my brother grabbing Naomi's hand and leading her toward the garage.

Fuck.

He tries to drive drunk every fucking time.

Not going to happen tonight.

"We can talk later," I say, brushing past her rigid body.

"I'm pregnant," she says.

FUCK.

I stop dead in my tracks. I spin on my heels staring down at Harlow's belly. She's wearing her usual skin-tight dress that hugs her body like a second layer of skin. Her stomach is flat. Not even a hint of a bump.

I close my eyes trying to focus on when the last time I had sex with her was. I know it's been months, but when was it exactly... I rush through my flings over the last couple of months, and then I remember. It was the end of Sebastian's Christmas break. Early January. I came back after the previous party got out of hand and he was arrested for drunk driving. I was pissed and needed to let off some steam. Harlow was who I let off steam on.

It was definitely January. It's April now. If she is pregnant, there is no way it's mine.

I open my eyes calmly. My body has been calm this entire time in fact. Hearing a woman say she's pregnant would send most men's balls straight up inside their body. It would stop their hearts along with their breathing. It would shatter their world so they couldn't think straight or fuck another woman for months, even after the baby was confirmed not to be theirs.

Hearing a woman say she is pregnant doesn't have the same effect on me. Not because I want a baby. I sure as hell am not ready to be a father. But because I've heard the line used too many times. Women think they can trap a King if they say they are pregnant. I don't fuck without protection. I don't knock up women. And if she were pregnant, all my money and prestige would go to the baby, not her. I don't want a relationship. That's not who I am.

I turn away from her, not bothering to give her another second of my attention. I need to find Sebastian before he ruins the King name, again.

"Well? You're really going to walk out on the mother of your child?" she says, grabbing my arm.

I exhale to keep from pummeling her. I'm so tired of this shit.

I turn and look at her with a glare, my nostrils flare, and my frown burrows. She takes a step back, her hand falling from my arm.

"My lawyer will go with you to your next appointment to confirm you are pregnant."

She smiles brightly. She's pregnant, or she wouldn't be so smug about it.

"And to take a paternity test."

Her smile drops, and fear flickers in her eyes. The baby isn't mine. I don't know if she can take a paternity test at this point, or if we'd need to wait until the baby is born. But I don't have to wait. Her eyes confirmed what she wouldn't tell me.

In some weird way, I wish she was pregnant. Not because I want to deal with Harlow Hill for the rest of my life, but because if I had a child, an heir to my inheritance, maybe it would stop other women from trying so hard to make me theirs. If they realized Harlow was getting noth-ing, and I planned on turning my entire empire over to my first born, maybe the harassment would stop.

I could put out in every interview I don't want a sibling for my child. I don't want children fighting over running my company the way Sebastian and I fought over my father's. Maybe all this chaos would stop. *Maybe having a child wouldn't be the worst thing in the world?*

My eyes bulge thinking about it. I've gone mad. Having

a child would destroy everything I've worked to build on my own.

I leave Harlow speechless, and I start jogging toward the garage, leaving my unfinished beer with a waiter on my way.

The Jaguar is gone. *Shit.*

Every. Fucking. Time.

I shake my head and run to my Aston Martin. My blood is boiling as I start the car up and zip out of the garage, dodging drunk college kids as I drive as fast as I can in the direction I know Sebastian drove.

He's predictable; I'll give him that. Why can't he be predictably responsible? The kind of kid who can throw a party without one issue. Where he fucks the women in his bedroom and passes out afterward. Like normal college students.

The lawyer I hired shouldn't have fought to scrub Sebastian's last DUI from his record. Sebastian should have lost his driver's license. Although, I doubt that would have stopped him. I should take his cars away, but he'd buy a new one.

I'm installing one of those breathalyzer tests on his cars so his cars won't start without him being sober. And since there are no sober people at his parties, he would never be able to leave.

My face burns red, and I grip the wheel tighter when I spot his red Jag on Highway 101, leading toward his favorite cliffside spot overlooking the beach. Naomi is in the passenger seat, and he has his arm draped around her back.

Why he thinks he needs to bring women here, I'll never understand. He's a King. Any woman at his party would fuck him. He doesn't need to be charming or sober. He can be sloppy drunk, barely able to get his dick up, and any woman at his party would praise him for how great the sex was.

I don't think he does this to impress the woman. He does this to piss me off. He hates me trying to control his life, and this is his fucked up way of trying to fight back. That, and he likes his fast cars almost as much as he likes his women.

I sigh.

I don't know how I'm going to let him take over any of my clubs. I want to give him one club. *One* single club. The one here in Santa Barbara. So there is no reason for me ever to return to this fucking town. And he can prove he is capable of doing more than finding trouble.

Then, I might let him run a few more parts of the business. *Maybe.* Or he'll decide he hates running a business and will live off his trust fund and name our father left us.

I stick my hand out the window, the chilly air cooling my warm skin. I try to calm myself down so when I beat Sebastian's ass when he stops, I don't break his nose like last time. Though he deserves worse.

Squealing breaks bring me back to reality.

Sebastian swerves.

I slow and pass him, as his car tumbles into the ditch on the side of the road. Flipping once and landing upside down.

I scream, my voice high pitched as I witness the accident.

I pull my car off the road in front of his wrecked car slamming on the brakes, and jump out, preparing myself for the worst. I sprint to the upside down driver's door.

I grab the door handle to open the door, but it won't

move. The window is open, but luckily it was too cold to put the top down, or this could be a lot worse.

I reach inside, undoing his seat belt.

"You okay, Sebastian?" I ask.

He coughs and smiles. "That was fucking insane!"

I exhale a breath I didn't realize I'd been holding. He's fine, just drunk. I pull him out of the car and inspect him for a second. He has a small cut above his eyebrow, but he seems fine. I'll call an ambulance after I check on Naomi so a doctor can check him out, and he's booked for drunk driving, again.

But he'll be fine, because as much as I want to kill him for being so stupid, he's still my brother. The only person who loves me. I won't let him rot in jail, or ruin his life for fucking up again. I will find a way to put an end to this. Even if it means taking away every one of his fucking cars.

When I ensure Sebastian is okay, I race over to the passenger side and pull the door open. Naomi has undone her seatbelt and falls into my arms smiling.

"That was wild!" she shouts, equally drunk and happy. I inspect her quickly, and she doesn't appear to have a scratch on her either. Which is good, because her family would definitely sue if she's injured. They will probably sue anyway, unless Sebastian agrees to marry her, or some shit like that.

I sigh, pulling my phone out to report the accident to the police, and call for an ambulance for the two crazy idiots that are now laughing, holding each other like they got out of the theater after watching a hilarious movie, instead of being lucky for surviving a car accident.

"911, what's your emergency?"

I exhale again, trying to remain calm. This isn't the time

for lectures. That will come tomorrow, when Sebastian's no longer drunk.

"I need to report an accident on Highway 101, just past exit seventy-one."

"How many cars are involved?"

"One."

"Can you tell if anyone was injured?"

"Both of the passengers in the car appear fine, besides a few minor cuts."

"The police and ambulance are on their way and should be there in…"

A moan grabs my attention, and I turn back around, ignoring the woman on the phone. I stare at Sebastian and Naomi who are both still cracking each other up. They didn't make those groans.

"Sir. What is your name sir? Any other information you can give me?" The woman keeps asking me questions, but I ignore her, pulling the phone from my ear as I move to the front of the car.

Moaning. It sounds like a woman's moan, and it sounds terrible.

I don't see anything, initially. I look under the front of the car and see nothing.

The moan grows louder. It hits my soul and sends me into a panic. There is someone out here.

My eyes scan the darkness, searching. I finally spot the white T-shirt reflecting the light from the Jags' headlights.

I run faster than I thought possible to her, bending down to a woman lying in the dirt on the side of the road. She's wearing nothing but a white T-shirt and underwear. Her toned legs stretch for miles. I would know her body anywhere.

Larkyn.

I search around for her bike or the car she was thrown from, but I find neither. She walked home. This is my fault. I should have made sure she got into a car, not walk on the side of a highway in the dark.

I grab the phone and pull it back to my ear.

"There is a woman injured. I think she was hit by the car while walking on the side of the highway," my voice is shaky as I speak.

"Is she conscious?"

"Larkyn? Can you talk to me?" I ask, tapping her gently on the shoulder.

A soft moan escapes her lips.

"She's not speaking, just moaning."

"I don't want you to move her. The ambulance is caught up in a storm, a tree fell blocking their way, but they should be there in less than ten minutes. Without moving her, check to see if you notice any obvious injuries."

My eyes water as they search over her body. She's injured, everywhere. Blood coats her skin, but I can't tell where it's coming from.

The operator said not to flip her over, but there is so much blood pouring around her body. I need to know. I flip her over, cradling her head as I do, to prevent any damage.

I see a massive piece of glass sticking into her stomach, along with smaller pieces of sticks and glass all over her body.

She moans again but doesn't open her eyes. Her breathing is frail and shallow. I check her pulse, and it's just as weak. I don't know what to do about the blood. If it's better to leave the glass in, or not.

"There is a large piece of glass sticking out of her

stomach and a lot of blood. She's barely breathing, and her pulse is weak," I tell the operator.

"Okay, stay with her and make sure she continues breathing but don't touch the glass."

"How much fucking longer?" I ask, knowing she won't make it much longer without assistance.

"Nine minutes."

My eyes widen as she strangles her breath. Her breathing stops for a second.

"Breathe Larkyn!" I shout, not allowing her to die in my arms.

The phone falls from my hands, and I glance over at my car, then Sebastian and Naomi. Both thankfully stopped laughing, realizing the seriousness of their fuckup.

The wind picks up, and I know it's going to be longer than nine minutes. Storms in this town come from nowhere, and destroy everything in their path. This is one of those times.

The hospital is five minutes away; less, if I drive as fast as I want to. I'm not waiting.

I scoop Larkyn into my arms and race toward the car.

"Get in the fucking car," I shout to Sebastian and Naomi.

They do, Sebastian sits in the back, holding out his arms to hold Larkyn, as I lower her into the car.

Her eyes flicker open at me, and I swear she peers into my soul at that moment. Then, they close again as if I imagined it.

"Make sure she's still breathing. If she stops, tell me," I shout at Sebastian as I hop into the driver's seat, speeding as fast as I've ever driven to the hospital. I hope Sebastian is now sober enough to notice if she is breathing or not.

Sebastian fucked up.

I fucked up.

And now Larkyn is paying the price.

She moans again, letting me know she's still breathing.

Thank fuck. Keep breathing Larkyn. I can't live with myself if you die.

4 LARKYN

A MACHINE BEEPS RHYTHMICALLY NEXT to my head. The sound isn't supposed to be heard. It's supposed to become background noise. But my headache controls me. It's as if you found all of the jackhammers in the world and used them all to drill into my head at the same time.

I'd take the jackhammers over what is happening in my head right now. My head is worse. A simple beeping is enough to make me want to rip off my ears and throw them at the machine, in hopes it will stop.

I keep my eyes closed, though I'm awake. Even with my eyelids shut, the light is too bright for my sensitive eyes to handle. Now I want to carve out my eyes, too.

Great, at this rate I won't have any body parts left.

"Larkyn, are you awake?" the evil bastard asks.

I lie still, hoping Kade will go away if he thinks I'm asleep.

"I saw you ball your hands into fists, and you frowned when you heard me speak, so I know you are awake. You might as well talk to me," the son of a bitch says.

Kade's not going away. He feels guilty for what

happened. That guilt won't go away if he leaves. Maybe if I talk to him, he'll leave.

"Turn off the lights," I say.

I swear I feel the bastard grin. "I'm that bad to look at, huh?" Kade asks.

My lips tighten, but I refuse to frown or show any emotion for Kade. He and Sebastian are cruel. They don't get to witness my suffering.

"No, I have a headache that hurts like a motherfucker, and the light is making it worse," I say, not adding I don't want him to see me in pain.

Kade turns off the lights without any more argument.

I slowly open my eyes. My eyes don't burn from the light, but I wouldn't call the room dark. The closed blinds let in far too much light to dampen how much agony I'm in.

Kade narrows his eyes at me and reaches out to touch my hand, as he sits on the edge of my bed. I pull my hand away and hide it under the covers so he can't attempt to touch me again.

"You're pissed, that's good," Kade says.

"How is being pissed a good thing?"

He smirks. "Because it means you remember what happened. The doctor was afraid you might not remember. The accident might have fucked with your head."

"Of course I remember your brother almost fucking killing me!"

He cocks his head. "And yet, you're looking at me like you want to kill me as well, even though I saved your life."

I huff and glare at him. I want both King brothers out of my life. I don't want to think about either of them again. I wouldn't be in the hospital for the dozenth time if it weren't for these assholes.

I glance at the door, afraid Sebastian is going to walk in

and want to apologize. I'm not ready for that. I don't want to see him. Ever.

"Don't worry, Sebastian isn't here," Kade says.

I exhale, after realizing I had been holding my breath.

"But Serena may walk in at any moment. She hasn't left you, except to get coffee and occasionally food when I demand she leave," Kade says.

I smile. At least I have one friend. But that means... If Kade knows Serena hasn't left my side, then he hasn't left my side either.

He looks at me with his big smoldering eyes, and my anger falls away. Kade did save my life, and then he stayed with me. I can hate his brother all I want, but I can't hate him.

Nope, definitely can't hate him when he's looking at me with hungry eyes.

I force my eyes away, and the bastard chuckles like he knows the effect he has on me.

"How are you feeling?" he asks.

"Like I got hit by a car."

He winces. "I'm sorry."

I sigh. Kade's sorry seems sincere. When he speaks, his whole body matches his mood. His eyes grow heavy, his voice softens, and his body stills.

"It's not your fault, but I feel like shit. I want to rip my head off..." I move to sit up more. "Fuck, that hurts." I grab my side.

He frowns. "You had a sizable piece of glass stuck in your large intestine. They removed the glass along with part of your intestine. They removed your appendix too."

My eyes widen. "What else?"

He blinks, and I swear I saw a tear there. "You have been unconscious for forty-eight hours. You have a concussion, that's why your head hurts so much. Glass in your stomach. Small shreds of glass in your legs, stomach, and head. A couple of broken ribs. Lots of internal bleeding. A couple of broken bones in your left wrist."

I look down and see the small cast on my left arm for the first time. *How did I not notice that?* Oh yea, because my fucking head hurts so badly I can't think of anything else.

"And a couple of broken bones in your ankle. The doctors were amazed you didn't break more bones."

The last part hurts the worst. Broken bones in my ankle. That will take forever to heal. I won't be able to run for months.

Tears.

Dammit.

No.

Kade holds my gaze, reaches out, and touches my hand over the covers.

I let him.

I need the comfort.

"The doctor wants you to stay in the hospital for another day or two. And then, she'll set you up with a rehab program to help you gain your strength back. She gave you pain medicine a half hour ago, but I can call her back if you want more?"

"No, thanks."

He runs his hand through his hair, and I permit myself to look at him closer. He's still wearing the suit he wore two nights ago. The collar is open with multiple buttons undone, revealing a chest that looks hot, dark, and delicious. Then, I see the red blotches. Blood. *My* blood.

"Do you want me to call your family? Your emergency contact lists Serena, so they called her. But she said she didn't have any of your family members' numbers, and they never found your cell phone."

"I didn't bring my cell phone. And, no." I don't offer him any more explanations. I sure as hell don't need my father lecturing me for walking home in the dark on a busy highway. If he finds out, I'll deal with the lecture later.

"Okay," he says, rubbing his neck.

My throat locks up, and my hand trembles a little in anger thinking about Sebastian, but I need to know. "How are Sebastian and his date doing?"

Kade moistens his lips and smiles softly. "Sebastian is a jackass, but he and Naomi are both fine. Sebastian was lucky, only a cut on his forehead requiring stitches. And Naomi has a little back pain from the collision."

I nod. I hate them, but I'm glad they aren't injured.

"Sebastian would like to apologize when you're ready to hear it. I told him that would probably be months or years from now. He understands. He's offered to give up his driver's license, and do some community service. He will also pay all of your hospital bills, and pay you well for your emotional damages."

The words Kade is speaking make sense, but I don't want to hear them.

"No, thanks."

Kade grimaces. "You can sue him, but you'll lose. Sebastian has a highly paid lawyer who doesn't lose. If you fight this, you will be out lawyer's fees and get no reimbursement. Sebastian won't lose his driver's license or do community service, and he definitely won't spend a night in jail, if that's what you are after, as much as he deserves it."

My eyes flicker to Kade's. Though he is defending his brother, his eyes say Sebastian deserves worse than he is getting.

"I'm not going to sue him. I don't want his money or apology or any of it. I don't want to think about Sebastian again."

Kade's body stiffens, and his face grows red before he pulls his phone out. "Make sure Larkyn's hospital bills are taken care of." Then, he ends the call.

I frown.

"You can't do that."

"I just did."

I sigh. I should let Kade pay my hospital bills. I don't have enough to cover them, and I don't want to have to go to my father for this.

"Paying for your hospital bills isn't enough though. What else can we do for you? Sebastian will do anything to make this right."

I peek under the covers and see the brace on my foot. I wince at the black and blue covering my legs. This accident is going to ruin my running career.

"He can't make this right. I don't want to be near him. And I sure as hell don't want his money."

"Then, let *me* make this right," Kade says, his head dropping a little in embarrassment.

"You did when you saved me."

He shakes his head. "That's not enough. I shouldn't have let you walk home that night. You wouldn't have been out there in the dark if I hadn't made sure you had a ride home, instead of treating you like crap. I'm sorry. Let me make it up to you."

Damn Kade, and his sincere apologies. His puppy dog eyes and sad face, which somehow still shows his dimples, make me want to grab his face and kiss him. Then accept his apology immediately. I restrain myself, mainly because moving that much would hurt like a motherfucker.

"Kade, I don't—"

"Stop, I'm making this up to you. I understand you don't want to deal with my brother, and you're right. He doesn't deserve to be forgiven any time soon. But let me be nice so that I can have a shot at forgiveness sometime in my lifetime."

He grins.

And I grin.

His grin reaches his eyes when he knows he's winning.

"I'm stubborn. I won't take no for an answer. So you might as well start thinking of ways I can help you."

I bite my lip, trying to stifle my smile, but it's a useless endeavor.

"Okay."

He tightens his grip on my hand over the covers, and I regret hiding my hand away in the first place.

"So what will it be? Money? A new car? A broken faucet that needs fixing?"

I raise an eyebrow. "You know how to fix a broken faucet?"

He shrugs. "I know how to hire a plumber."

I shake my head. Of course, his ways of helping are to give me money. I don't want his money, though. If I won't take my father's, I sure as hell am not taking a King's money.

What do I want?

To be healed, but Kade can't help me with that. He already covered my hospital bills.

I need a place to stay after graduation, but I don't want to take his money.

My car could use a tune-up, but no, no money.

Graduation is coming up. I could use a new dress for the graduation party my father is throwing, so for once, I could meet his unbelievably high standards. But again, that would require Kade's money.

My face lights up when the perfect idea creeps in. I shyly peek over at Kade. *Do I have the balls to ask him this?*

He's looking at me eagerly, squeezing my hand twice, trying to coax words out of my mouth. I don't have a choice but to ask him or come up with another way for him to pay me back, fast.

"My father is throwing me a graduation party in two weeks."

"Isn't that a bit early for a graduation party?"

I smirk. "Yes, but my father wants to throw it early, so he doesn't have to cancel and be embarrassed in front of his friends on graduation day if I don't graduate."

"Is that a possibility? I mean...don't answer that," he says, his cheeks flushing. He draws his hand back and grabs his neck, like his collar is too tight, though his collar is barely brushing against his neck.

I'm not offended by his words, so I continue, forcing the words out. "Take me to my graduation party, and pretend I'm yours for the night."

He sinks back in the chair next to my bed, like I pushed this conversation too far. But of course, I did. I asked Kade King to pretend to be mine for a night. It would ruin his reputation in Santa Barbara. If any of the wealthy women that run this town saw Kade King with me, the drama it would cause would never end. He can't go on a date with me. Even if it might be the only thing to make the disappointment in my father's eyes disappear.

"You mean, be your date for the night?" he asks.

I bite my lip again, considering not saying the next words, but I'm committed now. "No, I mean, pretend I'm your girlfriend for the night. It has to be more than just a date."

Kade's eyes narrow as he searches mine for the truth. For why I need him to pretend I'm his girlfriend. But he isn't going to find the truth. If he pretends to be my boyfriend, he might get answers. It would take him five minutes in my father's presence to figure out why I need him. But if he says no, he'll never know the reason for my embarrassment.

The silence stretches, and I can't take it any longer. If he wants to say no, he needs to say it and stop toying with my emotions.

"I understand," I say, but I can't continue. He should go.

"I'll pretend you're mine for as long as you want," he says, with a wink.

I chuckle. "The one night will be enough." I peer at his cocky grin and blush. I hope one night is enough.

5 KADE

LARKYN THINKS I'M AN ASS. She has no idea how amazing I can be as a boyfriend. I'm about to blow her mind.

I'm supposed to meet her at her parent's house for the graduation party they are throwing for her. *Not happening.* If I were her boyfriend, I wouldn't be meeting her anywhere. I would pick her up in one of my fancy cars, and drive her around proudly. So that's what I'm doing. If I'm going to pretend she's mine, I'm doing this right.

Shortly after noon, I park the car outside the apartment building she shares with Serena. Thank god I got Serena's number while waiting for Larkyn to wake up in the hospital. She told me where Larkyn lives, so I'm able to pull this off. I haven't talked to Larkyn in two weeks, since she woke up in the hospital. My throat feels dry just thinking about what condition she's going to be in. The last time I saw her, she was beaten up, broken. All I could focus on was her bruises and pain. I can't imagine that two weeks will have changed much. She may even need crutches or a wheelchair to get around.

I run up the stairs to their floor, holding the flowers in my hand with a smirk on my face. I thought Larkyn would want me to do something horrible to pay her back. Like, perform at a gay strip club. Or dress in drag. Something *creative*. Instead, when she said she wanted me to claim her as mine, it was like she granted my wish. She gave me an excuse to put my hands on her. To kiss her. Worship her. And I plan on cashing in on that excuse all night long.

I knock on the door with my smug grin, knowing that this simple gesture is sure to earn me big points with Larkyn.

The door opens, and instead of the smile I'm expecting, she frowns.

"What are you doing here? I told you to meet me at my house."

I roll my eyes. One thing I'm learning about Larkyn is she likes things her way. If she's going to be mine for the night, she needs to learn to let go, because I like doing things my way. And that includes bringing her flowers and driving her to the party.

I hold out the flowers, and she reluctantly takes the roses, unable to hide her growing smile behind the dark red flowers.

"You're my girlfriend for the night. If anyone saw us show up separately, the ruse would be ruined before the night even started."

She sighs. "You're right."

I grin. I like her saying I'm right. I finally take in her appearance. Her flawless skin is wrapped in a deep blue sundress that flares out at her hips and gives her just enough cleavage. I might have overdressed a little in my dark grey suit complete with a tie, but it doesn't matter. I'm sure she wants me as her date to make an ex-boyfriend jealous. Being more dressed up than everyone else will make my job easier.

My smile drops. Her skin is *flawless*. I don't see a bruise or a cut. Either she heals quickly, or she's wearing a ton of makeup. It was hard for me to look at her before when she was in the hospital. Not because the bruises and cuts made her appear ugly, but because they reminded me of my role in her suffering.

I glance down at her hands grasping the flowers, then dart down quickly to the heels on both of her feet. No cast or brace on either. No crutches. No wheelchair. I might believe the bruises healed enough to be covered in makeup in two weeks, but I know there is no way her wrist or ankle healed this quickly. The doctors said it would be weeks or months before the braces could come off, and even then it would be a long road of training and exercises before she was back to her old self.

She takes a step back, motioning me inside, and then curses as her ankle gives out in her heals. I grab her hips, keeping her upright.

"Are you supposed to be wearing heels right now? I thought your doctors said to wear your braces for a few more weeks?"

"She's supposed to be using her braces. But she's a stubborn ass that won't listen to anyone," Serena says, taking the roses from Larkyn's hands and storming into the kitchen to put them in a vase.

Larkyn half frowns, half grimaces from the pain. "I'm not going to my graduation party and letting everyone stare at me in the braces."

I narrow my eyes, not understanding why it would matter if she were wearing her braces or not. Surely, everyone would understand she is still healing from an accident that wasn't her fault.

"That's because they would ask questions since you haven't—" Serena stops when Larkyn shoots daggers her way with her eyes.

I look between the two women, even more confused at what's going on.

Larkyn continues inside, and I keep my hands on her waist, afraid she is going to hurt herself. It also gives me an excuse to be touching her.

"You should at least wear flats, those heels look dangerous," I say, staring at the high spikes on her feet.

Larkyn glares at me with a growl that tells me to shut the hell up.

I grin. I like that look.

"No, she should wear her braces," Serena says.

"Will you two stop? It's my choice. I feel fine. I'm not used to walking in heels, but after wearing them a few more minutes, I'll be used to them." She shakes my hands off her body as she storms over to the kitchen to pick up her purse and throw the strap over her head to cross her body. Her purse is a light tan color, not flashy, like Larkyn.

She stomps past me, without a word to Serena or me, merely an evil glare.

"Have fun!" Serena shouts from the kitchen. Then she looks at me. "Don't keep your hands off her. Larkyn's stubborn. She won't tell you she's in pain and she is in agony since she stopped taking her pain medications almost immediately after she got home. And she couldn't walk in heels before; she definitely can't now."

My eyes turn to the sassy woman strutting out of the apartment, her ass swaying making her flowy dress swoosh side to side as she walks. I much prefer the dress she was wearing the other night that hugged her body a little too snugly. This one makes her look as innocent as she is. This one will force me to behave like a gentleman, instead of the cocky bastard, I want to be.

"Don't worry, I won't be able to keep my hands off her," I say, winking at Serena who is smiling, amused.

Shit. I may have just given her the wrong impression about what my intentions are with Larkyn. I won't fuck her. I won't hurt her. I'm paying back my debt to her, that's it.

I need to talk to Serena on her own and explain things. And also receive some advice on how to convince Larkyn to take my money.

I chase after Larkyn as she reaches the stairs. Of course, she decided to skip taking the elevator. She's a wreck walking on a flat surface. I can't imagine how she is on the stairs.

I reach her as she is taking her first step down and hold out my elbow to her, like I'm escorting her down the stairs at some grand ball.

"What are you doing?" she asks, her body tense as if she might slug me.

"I'm being a good date. Now shut up and stop asking me that."

"You don't have to pretend until we arrive at the party. For now, can't we just be us? Friendly toward each other and nothing more?"

"No."

I grab her hand and place it on mine. I only get one day with her. I'm not wasting a second of it being *friendly* toward her.

She sighs but lets me help her down the stairs under the illusion I'm doing this because I'm pretending she's my date, instead of it being necessary to ensure she doesn't hurt herself.

I lead her to my McLaren, and she smirks when it comes into view.

"You couldn't pick me up in something nicer than this piece of trash?" she asks teasingly.

I smile. "Sorry, next time I'll pick you up in my horse and carriage, princess."

That earns me a smile, and I never want her to stop smiling. The smile reaches her deep eyes and makes the blonde in her hair shine. Her cheeks blush enough to be noticeable, but not so much that she appears embarrassed. Just happy. I haven't seen this look on her. I like it.

I open the door and help her inside, hating that I have to drop her warm hand to run around to the driver's side. I hop in quickly and throw my arm around her shoulders as I start driving toward the address she texted me to meet her at.

Her body tenses when I throw my arm over her shoulders. But she doesn't say anything. Maybe she'll finally give up, and try to enjoy herself a little. She might like being mine if she let herself benefit from the perks.

Her fingers fidget with the hem of her dress as I turn on the highway. I swear I hear her heartbeat speed to hummingbird levels. Her breathing catches in her throat. And her face turns pale white.

"What's wro—shit," I curse when I realize what's wrong. This is the same highway where my idiot brother ran her over and almost killed her.

I turn off at the next exit, almost running over a minivan, as she squeezes her eyes shut and grabs for anything to brace herself with. She finds my hand. And she grips it, as if she were to let go, she'd float away and get sucked up by a black hole.

My hand hurts like a bitch, but there is no way I would ever let her stop holding it. *Never.* I want her tiny hand gripping mine. I would take this over any of my usual daily activities in a heartbeat.

I pull the car over to the side of the road as she takes several deep breaths and stares out the windshield. Her grip slowly loosens, but I tighten my hand around hers, letting her know I'm not going anywhere.

Seconds pass. Or minutes. I don't know.

But finally, she turns her attention from staring at the field in front of us to me. Her big eyes are swollen as if she might cry, but won't let herself.

"I didn't realize how much driving on that road would affect me."

"I'm sorry. I wasn't thinking. I should have driven a different route."

She shakes her head. "I would have said you were crazy for taking a longer route when this was the most direct way. I'm stubborn like that. You would have driven on the highway, and only then would I have realized my mistake. I'm glad I was with someone the first time, instead of driving myself when the panic attack hit."

I grin, and reach over to her body, pulling her into my arms so I can hug her. She lets me. Exhaling another breath, this one goes deeper than her previous breaths, now that I'm holding her.

She gently leans back in her seat, and I reluctantly lean back in mine. But I still hold her hand, dammit. I'm not letting go.

"I'm better now. We should go if we want to make it to the party on time," she says, her voice steady.

I nod and start driving. "You're going to have to give me

directions. I don't know how to go anyway but the highway."

"Keep going straight. I'll tell you when to turn."

I do as she says, and the silence stretches out between us. It's not uncomfortable, but I don't want her thinking too much about what just happened.

"Tell me about yourself," I say.

She raises an eyebrow and makes a face like that's the worst thing I've ever suggested.

I laugh and bring her hand to my lips and kiss the top of it without thinking.

Her teeth rake over her bottom lip as she tries to pretend she didn't enjoy the simple kiss on her hand. But she did. She shivered when my lips touched her skin.

"I should know something about you if I'm going to pretend I'm your boyfriend for the day. What if someone asks me what your favorite food is or if you prefer red or white wine and I don't know the answer?"

She scrunches her face as she thinks a moment. "I rarely drink, but usually red wine, I guess, if I was going to choose. I don't have a favorite food either, and trust me, no one will ask. The basics are I go to UC Santa Barbara, and I'm graduating in two weeks with a business degree with a minor in finance. My best friend is Serena. I've lived with her all four years of college. We moved into the apartment last year. I love running. That's what I spend most of my time doing. And I teach yoga classes at the YMCA. And I don't bring guys home ever. So be ready for everyone to be shocked as hell at the sight of you."

She eyes me brightly with a goofy smile.

I blink rapidly, trying to take everything in. Except, all I can focus is on one thing. "How can you not have a favorite food? It's not possible. My favorite things are sex and pizza. Preferably together, but I'll take them separately."

She bursts into laughter. Most of the women I've dated, I've hated their laughs. Not Larkyn's, though. I love her laugh. It's not too high-pitched. It's not pretty either. She doesn't laugh while trying to bat her eyelashes at me or hide some of it to keep it feminine. Her laugh is deep and glorious.

"Sorry, I'm just imagining Harlow with cheese and marinara all over her body. And her annoyed face when some of the sauce reached into her hair. It made my day to think of her like that."

I narrow my eyes, amused at her. "How do you know Harlow?"

Her laughter stops, and her cheeks blush. "I may have looked you up. I thought the same thing; that I should know something about you if I was going to pretend you're my boyfriend. Harlow was in a lot of the pictures I found. Unfortunately, I didn't know much about you before that night, only Sebastian."

My heart hurts, and my throat growls.

Her eyes widen and stare at my neck.

I don't know why I growled, but I hate that she thought of my brother, and not me.

Her face changes. It lights up like the sun outside, whizzing by over the rolling hills. We haven't passed any houses or towns in a while. Hopefully, she's not taking me somewhere where she can push me off a cliff.

"Don't worry, I don't think you have to worry about me thinking about Sebastian like *that* ever again," she winks.

I sigh and try to forget about my brother. "So you think you know everything you need to know about me?"

She grins. "You graduated from Stanford four years ago.

You own several businesses. Real estate, whiskey line, but your love is the bars you own. You've dated, but don't seem to have a steady girlfriend. You're one of LA's sexiest bachelors according to the article with an accompanying naked picture." She wiggles her eyebrows.

I chuckle. "They didn't ask my permission to use that photograph!"

She laughs. "Why did a photograph exist where you were completely naked on a bed except for the sheets draped over your crotch?"

"I guess you don't know everything about me then."

She blushes, and her eyes alight like it's a challenge to figure out why I have the picture. If she figures it out, she won't like the answer. A woman took it after I slept with her. She just happened to be a photographer and sold it to the magazine. I didn't bother fighting it since it gave me and the business good press.

"What else do you know?"

"I know that the town loves you. You're a King. Your father left you an empire, and your mother left you when you were a kid. I know you have at least six cars and three homes across California."

"What about the important stuff? Like favorite food, drink, and sex position?"

That last part earns me a scowl, and she's as beautiful scowling as she is smiling. "Pizza apparently, scotch or whiskey I'd guess, but you'll be served neither at the party. My father's too cheap to serve anything like that. And sex position is any, as long as the woman is covered in marinara sauce."

I smirk and bring her hand to my lips again to kiss her.

This time she doesn't hide her smile. She reaches with

her other hand to turn on the radio, and it blares a country love song. She raises her eyebrows. "Really?"

I shrug. "I happen to like a good country ballad."

She turns the volume down. "Even this cheesy romantic crap about doing anything to win a girl back and driving down a country road in your truck?" She pauses. "You don't own a truck, do you?"

I chuckle. "I don't own a truck. And yes, I happen to like the cheesy shit."

I turn the volume back up and start belting along with Kenny Chesney.

She shakes her head like I'm crazy. I never ask her what music she likes, but I plan on finding out. Just like I plan on letting her know I like a lot more than cheesy love songs. I happen to like all things romantic. Romance is sweet; it's just not real.

———

I PULL up in front of her house, and my mouth drops. No way do her parents live here. I should have recognized the address. Some of the wealthiest families in Santa Barbara live here. It's not the most expensive house in this area, but it costs enough for me to be sure her family hangs in some of the highest circles of society. I'm surprised I didn't realize her family before.

Larkyn dresses like she doesn't come from money. Yet, she was relieved when I said I would pay her hospital bills, though she would never tell me that. Something doesn't add up.

She glances over at me and slowly pulls her hand out of mine. I let her pull away in my disbelief. *Dammit.*

"My parents are rich," she says shrugging. She's out of the car before I realize it.

I race after her to put my hand around her waist again.

"Stop running off on me. I'm your date, remember? Start pretending as if you like me."

She sighs. "Sorry, just distracted." Her body stands straight ahead in front of the large brick house with an arch over the front door and gorgeous deep pink flowers lining either side.

We go to the front door, and she rings the doorbell.

I study her. I thought this was her parents' house. This party is for her. *Why doesn't she just walk in?*

The door opens, and a gentleman dressed in a tuxedo answers it.

I thought I was going to be overdressed, but I'm underdressed. And Larkyn is way underdressed in her sundress.

Shit. I should have offered to buy Larkyn a dress for tonight if she didn't own one.

"Welcome, Miss Veil," the doorman says, holding the door out for us. "You're twenty minutes late, I believe."

She glares at him. "I know. And it's Larkyn Day. Call me Larkyn or if you insist, Miss Day. I'm not a Veil."

So many questions whiz around in my head, but at least one is answered. The reason I didn't recognize Larkyn came from money is that her last name doesn't match her parents'. The Veils have as much money as my father did. I didn't realize they had two daughters. Just—

"Anastasia," Larkyn says to her sister, who looks nothing like Larkyn.

Anastasia is wearing a sparkly red dress showing off voluptuous curves I happen to know she bought. I know because I've slept with her. *Shit. Shit. Shit.*

I try to hide my face by turning away from Anastasia

and hoping she doesn't notice or remember who I am. She was pretty drunk that night. That night is one of the reasons I instated my don't date anyone from this town rule.

"Hello, Larkyn. It's nice to see you *finally* made it to the party our father is throwing in your honor. You would think you would be one of the first to arrive," Anastasia says.

I hate her. We are twenty minutes past when the invitation said to arrive. Most people come after the invitation time to a party.

I grip Larkyn closer to my body, knowing she needs the support if she's going to survive her horrible sister.

Larkyn leans into me, and she takes a deep breath against my chest, ignoring her sister.

"Where is our father?" Larkyn asks.

"Smoking a cigar. He needed something to calm his nerves after thinking you might not show up." Anastasia steps toward her sister glaring at her, still ignoring me. "But don't worry, I will be announcing a surprise to liven this party up."

Larkyn scowls. "Good, then the party can be all about you instead of me."

Anastasia smirks and notices the arm wrapped around Larkyn's body. She looks up at me, and she laughs.

"You always did go after my sloppy seconds," Anastasia says before brushing past us, still laughing.

Silence.

"What did Anastasia mean about sloppy seconds?" Larkyn asks, her body rigid as she forces her lips upward as guests walk by.

I can't lie. There is no point anyway.

"I slept with Anastasia in college."

She nods like she knew the answer.

"Great. Just great."

She struts forward confidently, and I know there is no way she is going to fall in her heels, not now. My hand slips from her side momentarily, before I catch back up. She takes two glasses of white wine from the waiter because white wine and champagne are the only options waiters are serving at this party. Then she dashes off out back, with me at her heels.

Five minutes pass without her talking to me. She hides in the corner at the backyard, sipping her wine and sculling. Hating me. Loathing her sister. And hiding from the party.

"I'm sorry. If it makes you feel any better, Anastasia was horrible in bed. It only happened once because we were drunk. And if I had seen you first, she wouldn't have been an option."

That makes her smile though she tries to hide it. "You're lying, but knowing she's bad in bed does make me feel better."

"She was awful, one of my worst lays. All fake, and she thought all she had to do was lie there and let me do all the work. Not that I mind being on top, but give me something. Kiss me, touch me, moan, anything," I say, probably pushing this too far.

Larkyn bites her lip and is silent as she stares at me with her big eyes. "I don't think I need any more details. Picturing the two of you together isn't exactly making my day better."

She takes another sip of her wine, and her gaze catches the attention of a herd of chatty women in sparkly floor-length dresses. It's Larkyn's party, but they give her nasty glares as they judge her sundress, appropriate for most graduation parties in the world, except in the world of snobs in this town. To these people, a dress like the one Larkyn is wearing is meant to be worn at casual events, not for a special occasion.

Larkyn's eyes drop, and she winces then curses under her breath. I'm not sure if it is because she is pissed at the women, or if her leg is aching again. She lifts her injured leg up and rests it on top of her other foot. She finishes her wine, planning on getting drunk to deal with both her pain and the disgusting stares.

I have a better idea.

I finish my wine, though the stuff is disgustingly sweet.

"Come on. I may not be able to take away the torment you are dealing with in your leg unless you let me take you home and forget about the party."

She snaps her head to me. "Not going to happen."

I nod. "But at least let me help you with your other problem."

"I don't have any other problems," she lies.

I link my fingers in her hands again, and she shivers. I'd smile, but I'm too pissed off. Yet, I do love how much something so simple affects her. I bet I could ask her any question right now and she'd answer because she's too focused on my thumb lazily tracing the outside of her hand. I don't know how many boyfriends she's had in her life, but none of them have known what to do with her body, that much is clear.

I take my time as she hobbles in pain across the grass to where the women are watching us with narrowed eyes like they can't figure out who I am.

Every time she winces or curses, I press a little further to a pressure point in her hand. Her hand warms, and she stops groaning in pain every time I do. Every curse earns her a kiss on the hand. Both the touch and the kiss seem to help because by the time we approach the women, she's smiling and I know that at least part of the smile is genuine.

"Hello, ladies. How do you know the woman of the hour?" I ask, pulling Larkyn against my side as I wrap my arm around her waist. I want to do a lot more, but that won't win over these kinds of women. These women already look at her like she's trash. I won't add to the stereotype it's clear these women are giving her.

"Oh, we've been best friends with her mother and father since before she was born. You know how families like ours run together forever. How do you know Miss Veil?" one of the women asks for the group. But everyone peers over their drinks, none of them recognizing me. *But then, why would they?* I rarely ever come back to this town.

I'm not going to convince these women by playing their games. They are too good, and Larkyn hasn't been playing for years if she ever played at all.

"I'm Kade King."

Eyes widen, and whispers ring out.

I grin. I have their attention now.

"I'm so glad you are back in town Mr. King. I don't think you've met my daughter, Aubrey, yet. I'll fetch her," the woman says.

I smirk. I'm sure the woman would like to introduce me to her daughter. But it's not happening.

Larkyn is glaring at the women. Pissed. I think she's angrier at them than she was at Sebastian.

I tug on her hand, watching her stumble in front of me for a second, so I have an excuse to pull her tight against my body. Pressing her back to my front. My cock grows uncomfortably hard in this position. But I'll deal with the pain.

"Down girl," I whisper into Larkyn's ear, before kissing her tenderly on the neck.

A moan escapes, and my dick is never becoming soft again. It's going to be hard the rest of the fucking night.

"Larkyn is my girlfriend," I say, kissing her cheek.

She closes her eyes as I do, and when she opens them again, her eyes are fierce balls of furry, ready to fight anyone who argues we are anything other than boyfriend and girlfriend.

My statement earns us more whispering and stares. I'm not sure if it helped Larkyn or not, but damn does it feel great to say, even if it's not the truth.

"That's nice. But really, you should meet Aubrey. She's graduating from law school in a couple of weeks, and I think the two of you would hit it off," the woman says.

My mouth drops open. I grew up in this world, with women like her. It's one of the reasons I hate this town. I'm tired of daughters pushed on me.

"That's nice, Mrs. Jackson. And feel free to introduce Aubrey to Kade. Maybe she can date him when I'm finished with him. She'll be waiting a long time though. Because I don't plan on giving him up, ever," Larkyn says, storming away, her hand interlocking with my hand automatically as she pulls me away.

I chase after her willingly.

She stops just before we make it to the pool area, which is surrounded by a younger crowd.

"I'm so sorry. I don't know what I was thinking. I'm just so tired of never being enough for these people. Of course, we aren't going to keep this ruse up forever. After today, you are free to date Aubrey or anyone else you are interested in. I can't stand that they always get to win."

I tuck a strand of her curls behind her ear. She wore her hair down, unlike most of the women here. She doesn't understand she's the most beautiful woman at the party. She's not afraid to be herself, while everyone here is too worried about impressing others to think for themselves.

"Don't worry about it. If you hadn't said it, I was going to. I can't stand for them to win either. After today is over, we will find a way to make our breakup epic. We will find a guy for you to date who is way better than me," I say, not liking the words spilling from my mouth.

She smiles weakly. "Thank you."

I nod.

Gripping her hair a little firmer now, I watch as she closes her eyes and her face molds to my hand.

Her eyes flicker open a second later when I stop. Mortified.

"I'm sorry. Did I just moan? I don't know what's gotten into me," she says, with pink cheeks.

The same thing that seems to have stirred my dick up, and won't calm down. I'm surprised she hasn't noticed. If she has, she hasn't commented on it or stared.

I hear the laughter from the crowd behind us. We may not be able to win with the older group, but the younger ones will be easier to convince. And if she has an ex-boyfriend here, that's where he'll be.

"Let's have some fun," I say, with playfulness in my eyes and grin.

She cocks her head to the side as I pull her quickly toward the crowd. She tries to keep up, but she can't in her heels on the uneven grass. So I scoop her up, making sure her dress is still covering her ass as I run with her in my arms toward the crowd that is now silent.

They are all staring at us. Studying us, to determine what is going on. Now is the time to make the biggest show I can.

She's laughing, but it's not enough.

I grab her neck and pull her lips to mine. We kiss. I intended to keep it pure. Innocent. Our lips mashing together, but nothing else. That went away the second her moist lips touched mine.

Her lips part for me, and I can't not jump at the invitation. I slip my tongue into her mouth, not expecting her to be good at kissing. *But damn. She knows how to kiss.*

Her tongue dances with mine as she makes soft whimpers against my lips. Her hands tangle in my hair. And my cock presses harder into her body. There is no hiding how she makes me feel now.

Larkyn slowly ends the kiss, somehow having more restraint than I do. There is a twinkle in her eye when she cocks her head to the side laughing. She loved that damn kiss as much as I did.

She mouths thank you.

But I don't want her to thank me. I want her to want me. I want this to be real. I could use a hot fling with someone as innocent and pure as her instead of dealing with the experienced wenches that only want two things: to bear my children and steal my money.

I hear the hooping and hollering from the guys. I feel the shocked expression and whispers from the girls. They believe the act. My dick has decided our show is more than just pretend too.

I need a distraction if I don't want to walk around all night with a hard-on. And we need a grand finale to cement in their minds our relationship status.

I give her a warning with my eyes.

"No," she squeals.

And then I toss us into the pool.

When we come up for air, Larkyn is laughing, and I pull her to my body to kiss her again.

Her lips taste even better now that her body his soaking wet, and fully pressed against my body. Other people start jumping in now that we have. She smiles against my lips, knowing she is now a hit, at least with the younger crowd. They've all been secretly dying for a chance to dive into the pool all day.

"Larkyn," a stern voice says over us, and my body freezes. I think my balls climb up in my body a little at the sound.

Larkyn sighs, like she was waiting for this to happen, but she doesn't try to wiggle out of my arms.

"Hello, father," she says, staring up at a man.

I follow her gaze. I'm used to fathers glaring at me with unease and trepidation. I'm used to them eyeing me suspiciously, not sure if they like me with their daughters. But then when they realize who I am, they are doing everything they can to impress me.

But I'm not sure meeting her father while soaking wet was my best idea. I just needed a distraction from what she was wearing to keep everyone from thinking too hard about us. Now it seems stupid.

"Are you going to introduce your friend and spend some time with your family at your party? Or are you just going to play, instead of handling your responsibilities, as always?" her father says.

Larkyn takes my hand and leads me to the stairs of the pool, where she climbs out, kicking her heels off on the top step. I guess the heels don't matter now she's soaking wet. She doesn't seem pissed at me for putting her in this predicament though.

Her father starts walking into the house, and we follow. I snatch a towel off one of the chairs and wrap it around Larkyn, who gives me a curt smile and her own warning stare before we head into the house.

Her father is now standing next to, what I presume is,

her mother. Both dressed to the nines, while we are dripping on their marble floors. *Shit. Stupid.*

I open my mouth to start charming her mother. I know I can at least handle that, but Larkyn squeezes my hand, and I stop. She wants to handle this. I'll let her, as long as she includes the part where I'm her boyfriend.

Her father eyes me again as he puts his hand around his wife, pulling her to him uncomfortably.

"Mom, dad, this is Kade King, my boyfriend," Larkyn says.

Her mother smiles and her dad stiffens. I wasn't brought here to make an ex-boyfriend jealous. I was brought here to stick it to her parents.

I grin widely as I pull Larkyn to me and kiss her on the cheek.

"You've raised a wonderful daughter, Mr. And Mrs. Veil. And you have a beautiful home."

"Thank you," Mrs. Veil says.

Larkyn's father ignores me though and stares at his daughter. He shakes his head disappointedly, which confuses me.

Anastasia decides to join in on the fun, with a man in tow who looks like a sad puppy following his master's orders. They stand silently by, watching the exchange.

Larkyn stares her father down, daring him to deny we are dating.

"It's nice to meet you Mr. King, but can I offer you a piece of advice?" he asks, but it isn't a question. And he doesn't look at me when he speaks. He looks at Larkyn.

"Find another girl to date. Larkyn is only dating you for your money. I won't give her any money unless she gets a grown-up job, which she can't get without a degree. She thinks she doesn't have to work. Work is beneath her. She's just a spoiled, rich girl who will take everything you have without giving anything in return. She'll live off your money until there is nothing left. Larkyn is like her mother in that way," he says.

I see red. I've never punched anyone before, but right now I want to. I've only known Larkyn for a short period, but I know that almost every word he spoke is untrue. She doesn't care about my money. She wouldn't even take it when she should have. I don't know how smart she is. I don't know if she will graduate or get a job after college, but I know she is fully capable of taking care of herself.

I open my mouth to yell at the man when I realize Larkyn is ready to defend herself.

Her mother, on the other hand, looks bored. Likes she's heard this conversation too many times to care anymore.

Anastasia is smiling smugly, behind her father.

"Excuse me, I need to talk to my father. Alone," Larkyn says, pulling out of my arms.

I grab her hand at the last second, jerking her to me so I can taste her lips one last time, and prove to her father I am her boyfriend. That I'm not letting her go easily.

She gets lost in our kiss, forgetting her family is here until her father clears his throat.

She lowers herself down, after having to stand on her tiptoes to kiss me. I think I could get used to our height difference. Her body is so tiny I could easily throw her around in bed.

She walks away confidently, without any sign of the trauma that occurred to her body.

I'm left standing with the rest of her family. Her mother turns away to the bar to grab another drink, leaving me alone with Anastasia and her date.

Nope, I'm not going to stay around and make conversation with this bitch.

I follow after Larkyn, so I can be near whenever she finishes talking to her father. She might need comforting after dealing with him. I thought my father was an asshole; this man is just as bad or worse.

They dart into what I assume is an office, and Larkyn gives me a thank you, but I got this smile and wink before closing the door behind her, leaving me alone in the hallway still dripping wet.

I really don't know what I was thinking.

I remove my jacket, now ruined, along with my tie, and start unbuttoning my shirt as I eavesdrop on the conversation behind the door.

I can't hear everything, but I do hear...

You're broke.

No job.

No degree.

No future.

Kade isn't going to save you. You're not worth the trouble.

All words spoken by her father. He's yelling. Her voice must be softer, calmer because I can't hear a word she is saying.

I sigh.

She needs me more than I thought. She needs me more than just for tonight.

I swallow hard, rubbing my neck, trying to figure out what to do next.

Anastasia walks over and places her hand on my bare chest. "Too bad we never got a second chance. We were good together."

I frown, grab her hand, and remove it from my chest

before she touches the priceless piece of jewelry that always hangs from my neck.

"Any chance we could work out if we gave it another shot?" she asks, moving her hips side to side as she bats her eyelashes at me.

"I thought you were here with a date?" I ask.

"I am, and he's great. Tall, handsome, rich. Just not as rich as you." She says *you* with a raspiness to her voice meant to seduce me.

"No." I don't give her any of the other words I'm thinking. I'm sick of women acting like this around me because I'm wealthy. I need to find a solution to my problem.

She sighs. "Too bad. Oh well, make sure you and Larkyn get a good seat to my announcement."

"Announcement?" I ask although I remember her mentioning something about a surprise earlier.

She nods. "We have big news we're sharing in about fifteen minutes if father ever gets done lecturing Larkyn. I don't know why he wastes his time talking to her. She's never going to listen. She's a lost cause. I don't know why my family decided to adopt her in the first place.

"My mother thought I needed a sister, I guess, and she didn't want to fuck up her plastic surgery to have a second child of her own. So instead, she picked up some trash off the street and expected her to flourish in our world. Oh, well. She's not our problem anymore."

Anastasia rests her hand on my bare chest again, while I burn with rage.

"What the hell is wrong with you?" I spat out.

She grins. "Don't even try to defend her. I know the two of you aren't actually together. I saw her at Sebastian's party. I heard about the car accident. This is a pity date. Nothing more. Call me when you want a real woman," she winks before walking off, but not before I spot the flashy diamond on an important finger.

Shit.

Anastasia is going to announce she's engaged at Larkyn's graduation party.

Not fucking happening.

I stare at the door, trying to come up with a plan to ruin Anastasia's night and make Larkyn's.

I grasp for the ring hanging around my neck on a gold chain, as I always do when I need comfort.

And a solution forms. One I'm not sure if Larkyn will ever agree to. But it's the perfect plan. One that will solve both of our problems. Women will no longer hit on me. And Larkyn will be able to show up her family and get everything she's ever wanted. Money, security, and affection.

I need a few things. New clothes here, fast. And a diamond ring. Good thing I always carry a diamond ring with me.

6 LARKYN

"YOU CAN'T LIVE off your winnings as a runner! You'll never make enough money. And don't think I haven't noticed you're practically limping. Did you injure yourself again? How do you expect to be a good runner if you keep injuring yourself?" my father yells.

I pull the towel tighter around my body, trying to hold myself back from attacking as I want. My father doesn't know about the car accident. None of my family does. And I don't plan on telling any of them.

"I'll make enough. I'm still working as a yoga instructor. I'll be able to work more hours when classes are over next week. I'll survive."

He shakes his head, hanging it low like he can't even look at me. "You shouldn't just get by. You should find a real job. One in the business field, after you hopefully graduate."

"Stop. I'm graduating in two weeks. Just stop saying that."

"Fine. I'll accept you are graduating with a degree you will never use. What good is that? You have the skills, but won't use them? You'll be homeless or live off a man!"

I narrow my eyes. He has no idea what I want. He has no idea who I am or what my plans are.

"I won't be homeless or live off a man! I will make enough money to feed myself and put a roof over my head. That's all that matters. I don't care about money. I want to make a difference in people's lives." And I do, I just haven't figured out how I'm going to make a difference yet or what I want to do. All I know is I like running and helping other people stay fit. But I know it won't be sustainable to do forever.

"You can't make a difference without money. Charities, foundations run on money. So work hard at a big corporation, make your money, then start something like everyone else."

"No, I don't want to work at a big corporation."

Dad throws his hands up. We've had this same argument thousands of times before. I thought tonight with Kade on my arm he might stop. He might let me enjoy the night, but it made no difference.

He walks over to the bar and pours himself a drink as always. This is how he handles things. He drinks.

I won't stay another second and watch him drink his problems away. Drink *me* away.

I'm done.

I turn and storm out the door without a goodbye. The door swings open so hard it bounces back a little.

I expect Kade to be standing right outside the door waiting, but I don't see him. If he's with Anastasia, I'll chew him out too.

I turn down the hallway, and the AC hits my still soaking wet body. When I find him, I'll have him take me back to my apartment. I tried to make this day better, but it's impossible to do. If I don't find Kade soon, I'll call an Uber to take me home. I may not be able to afford it, but this is one of the few times I need to make an exception and figure it out because I can't stand being here for another minute. I have sixty-seconds to find Kade, and then I'm out of here.

I glance up and see Kade walking down the hallway toward me. He's not wet. He's changed clothes and is now wearing an even more dashing suit. This one is a dark blue and makes his grin shine. And he's holding something sparkly draped over his forearm.

I smile when I see him. Bringing him here may have been a horrible way for him to pay me back, but at least I got to spend some time with a great guy. I thought he was an asshole just like his brother, but he genuinely is a nice guy, even if he does date around too much. Maybe I've at least gained a friend out of all of this.

His arms wrap around my body when we meet, and his lips come down on mine. Passionately, not holding back, like I've been gone for days instead of minutes. His kiss is desperate for more, and as my lips part, I realize I never want him to stop kissing me. I didn't think it was possible for a man's kiss to ruin all other kisses for me. I've been kissed plenty of times, and they all had the same effect on me because they were pretty much all the same.

Kade's kisses, though, awaken parts of my body I didn't know existed. I feel *everything*. Excitement. Passion. Need. Ache. All of it. And I want what his kisses promise.

Then, I remember this is fake. He's kissing me because he's doing me a favor. Someone must be watching if he's kissing me.

He gently stops the kiss, his thumb tracing across my lips that are parted and useless after he devoured them.

"Your father was watching," he says, answering my unasked question.

I nod. I knew that's why Kade kissed me, but I just wish once he'd kiss me because he wants to. I don't need more than that, but I need to know on some level this was as real for him as it is beginning to be for me. I can't separate the pretend from how he makes my body feel. Which is very, very real.

He pushes the silky white fabric into my hands.

"What's this?" I ask.

He smirks, and puts his hands in his pockets, trying to act innocent. "Your new dress."

I stare at the beautiful white dress, decorated with gray lace and sparkles. I run the fabric through my hands, and it feels as good as it looks. It's meant to be worn, but I could just as easily use the heavenly fabric as a blanket in bed it's so soft.

"No, I just want to go home."

He narrows his eyes, determined as he grins at me. "I don't have time to argue with your stubbornness. I know today hasn't been perfect, but I have a plan to make it a whole heck of a lot better. We don't have a lot of time; I spilled wine on Anastasia's dress, but I know as soon as she's changed she will be ready to make whatever stupid announcement she's making. So hurry, and get changed."

I stare down at the gorgeous dress I would love to squeeze my body into. I know it would make me feel beautiful, and I need that right now.

"How did you get a dress so fast?"

He shrugs. "I have a friend in the fashion industry. He owes me plenty of favors, and was able to get a dress here quickly."

I try to think of the cons of changing into the dress. It means I'll have to stay, for at least a little while. I'll have to listen to Anastasia announce her engagement. I saw the ring. I know that's what she's planning. But if I have to listen to her steal the spotlight away from me, then I should at least do it feeling beautiful instead of like a wet mop.

"Fine. I'll change, and give you fifteen minutes to make this better. Then, we are leaving. Deal?"

He cocks his head to the side and smiles brightly. "Deal."

I rush into one of the spare bedrooms and change into the dress. It fits me better than any item of clothing I've ever worn. I don't know how Kade was able to get a dress here that is not only my size but tailored to my body.

I ring out my hair, letting my wet hair curl however it is going to curl. And I apply a little lipstick I find of my mother's in the adjoining bathroom.

I step back and stare at myself in the mirror. I look a little like a bride in the white dress. But I don't care. I love how I look. I look like a beautiful woman, instead of a girl playing dress up. I might even stay until the party ends to enjoy the dress longer.

I step back into the hallway where Kade is pacing back and forth. He freezes when he sees me, and his mouth drops open. And I swear I see his cock harden in his pants. Maybe it's just my wild imagination, but I like to think I'm the one causing his package to grow.

"What do you think?" I ask, twirling around like a little girl.

His hands reach my waist as I spin, and he stops me. His eyes rake up and down my body.

"Beautiful."

I lick my lips wanting another kiss but knowing I'm not going to get one. I don't think I've ever heard a man call me beautiful before. And it feels damn good.

He tucks his hand gently around my neck and under

my hair, staring intensely into my eyes before his lips press firmly against mine. I don't think about why he's kissing me. I don't search for anyone lurking in the hallway that might be the reason for the kiss. I just exist in a world where Kade King is kissing me because I don't want to ever live in any other world.

He stops, grinning against my lips. "That kiss was because I couldn't not kiss someone as beautiful as you."

My heart dances and my legs turn to mush as my body begins dropping to the floor. He holds me up like I'm a rag doll.

He grins wider, showing off his dimples beneath his five o'clock shadow that is beginning to form.

"I'd carry you, but then I'd take away from everyone getting to see how gorgeous you are in your dress."

I swallow and force my legs to work so I can stand. My legs are strong, muscular. Even if my ankle is in constant agony, my legs should be able to hold me up. I shouldn't need to rely on Kade to hold me up. But when I'm around him, my body forgets how to do anything other than kiss. I'm surprised I can still breathe without a constant reminder.

His hands slowly move down my side until he finds my hand and interlinks our hands.

"Come on, now for step two of my brilliant plan."

I laugh. "I'll be the judge of your plan after this is all over."

He shrugs. "How am I doing so far?"

We step outside to the patio near the gardens where everyone gathered. They stop talking and stare at us when we step out looking like a bride and groom on their wedding day. I know I won't ever look this good again, even on my wedding day, so I better enjoy this. There is no telling how much money this dress costs. Thousands of dollars at least.

"Pretty good," I say weakly, not sure how I feel about being the center of attention.

"My daughter and her date finally decided to join us," my father says, and everyone chuckles.

He raises his champagne glass as Kade and I am given our own champagne glasses by the waiter to match everyone else outside.

"I'd like to make a quick toast to my daughter Larkyn. To her new life after graduation. May she find her way, and not back under my roof."

The last part earns him chuckles, and everyone clinks their glasses as they drink to his toast. I've suddenly lost my ability to want to drink.

"To new beginnings. May you find a way to shove it to all these high-class idiots who don't know how amazing you are," Kade whispers in my ear, as he clinks his glass with mine.

I smile and drink my glass until it's empty. When I look up, I realize Kade has done the same. I don't know how many drinks he's had, but he better be able to drive me home later. I won't admit to him, but I enjoyed riding in his McLaren.

Anastasia grabs her fiancé's hand and starts to pull him forward as she glances at our father to let him know she's ready to make her announcement.

He smiles at her because of course, he's happy his princess has found love. But if I were announcing I was getting married, he'd think I was a gold digger who doesn't want to work.

"I think we should go. I changed my mind. I can't watch this, no matter how beautiful I feel," I whisper into

Kade's ear, pulling his hand to lead him out of here quickly. I don't care if Anastasia knows why I'm leaving, I can't stay.

Kade kisses the top of my hand, and I'm thankful he's going to go without a fight.

A hand tugs me to the center of the crowd with Kade being the one forcing me in.

I glare at him, not liking whatever he's doing.

He flashes me his handsome grin and gives me a tiny wink.

I can't help but stop protesting when he looks at me like he is now.

"Thank you, Mr. Veil, for your toast, but I'd like to offer one of my own. My toast is to the most wonderful woman I've ever met. To a woman, I'm desperately in love with, and can't imagine living without."

I bite my lip to keep from grinning at his fake words. I don't care that they are fake. I love hearing them. I could live in this fantasy world forever. Even deal with my stupid family and their friends if it meant hearing him say such wonderful things about me.

"I love you so much, Larkyn. You're beautiful, smart, feisty, stubborn. And I couldn't have built a more perfect woman for myself if I tried. I've been searching for a woman like you for a long time. And I kick myself every day for not finding you sooner, especially when you were this close to me."

His words have a bit of truth to them, even though I know he means as friends. He's sad we weren't friends earlier. I am too, but I'm sure we will keep in touch after this day is over and make up for lost time.

Kade holds my hand tighter, as he bends down on one knee.

My eyes widen staring at him, and the crowd gasps all at once at the sight of him on one knee.

He pulls something out of his jacket pocket. But I can't focus on the object, all I can do is stare into his eyes and try to figure out what the hell is happening.

"Larkyn Day, I love you. Marry me?"

Yep, he's lost his damn mind.

He's smirking, and I know he thinks he's come up with the perfect plan to stop Anastasia. And he has. I just don't think he's thought this through. He's making my dreams come true today, only to crush me tomorrow. We aren't in love. We aren't getting married. This is all a ruse. And tomorrow it will all be over. We can keep pretending for a while, but we aren't getting married.

He winks at me though, and I can't help but go along with his ridiculous plan. Even if it's going to hurt me tomorrow, it will be worth it today.

"Yes," I say, barely getting the words out.

"She said yes!" he shouts so the crowd can hear my answer.

Cheering and applause break out, and Kade stands up and slips a ring onto my finger. *Where the hell did he get a ring?*

And then he kisses me. Hard. Long. A kiss that makes me forget this isn't real. That Kade King isn't mine. And I'm not his.

But today, I am.

When the kiss ends, people begin hurriedly approaching us, bombarding us with questions, and ogling the ring I haven't even had the chance to look at myself.

"Oh my god! Look at the size of the ring. Is it eight carrots or ten?" the woman stares at Kade.

He smirks. "Ten."

My eyes come unglued as I stare at him. *How the hell does he have a ten carrot engagement ring for a fake proposal?*

He shrugs at me knowing I have a lot of questions for him. I know he's rich and has a lot of friends. That's apparently how I'm wearing this expensive dress right now. But I don't care how many friends he has in the jewelry business. No one would lend him this expensive of a ring for one day, on this quick of a notice.

"Excuse me. I need to thank my fiancé. *Privately*," I say winking at them, knowing I just caused a new wave of gossip as they think I'm about to take Kade into one of the bedrooms to fuck him.

I grab Kade's hand, and I pull him into the house, but people continue to follow us in. As much as I like sticking it to my sister and family, I'm done with being the center of the attention and the reason for the gossip.

So I keep guiding Kade out the front of the house, and this time, he doesn't argue or pull me back to the crowd that has now gathered outside of the house.

"Thank you all for coming to celebrate our engagement and Larkyn's graduation. We would love some time to celebrate before we decide on a date. But it will be soon," Kade says, winking at the crowd that is asking us questions about when the wedding will be.

Kade opens the door to his car and helps me inside, before jumping in himself and speeding off.

I hit him playfully on the shoulder. "You're so bad. Why did you let them think there is going to be a wedding soon? And oh my god!" I grab the ring off my finger and thrust it into his hand.

"I can't be wearing a ring this expensive. If I lose it, I'll be paying you back my entire life. I'll have to sell my kidney to make a down payment on paying you back."

He smirks, pulls over abruptly, and shoves the ring back onto my finger.

"Did you hear me? I can't afford to pay you back if I lost this ring."

"I know. It's not on loan."

I narrow my eyes.

"How did you get the ring then? Please tell me you didn't steal it off of someone's finger when they weren't looking."

He laughs. "No, it belonged to my mother."

Shit.

"I can't wear it, it's irreplaceable," I say, trying to get the ring off, but it's now stuck on my swollen finger. *Great.*

I feel the panic rising in my chest.

"Stop," he says, holding onto my hand.

I freeze. If I don't move, there is no way I can lose the ring.

"I want you to wear the ring."

"Why?"

"Because I want to pretend marry you."

KADE'S LOST his damn mind.

Or he's drunker than I thought.

Or maybe he's high?

Except, he doesn't seem any of those things.

He's sitting in the driver's seat next to me, waiting for me to speak. But he's been waiting a long time; I've yet to find my voice or ability to move at all.

All I can do is stare down at the gorgeous ring that weighs heavy on my finger. Ten carats was what the woman said. That's *insane*. If I'm going to do this, I have to convince him at least to buy me a cheaper ring to wear, because I can't wear a ring this expensive or this sentimental to him.

What am I doing? I can't be seriously considering this. This is crazy! I don't even know why he would want to do this. He hardly knows me. He doesn't want to be fake married to me.

Kade grasps my hand again and pulls it to his luscious lips, planting a small kiss on the palm of my hand before interlinking our fingers together.

I close my eyes as the familiar tingling crawls up my arm and races through my body. It's such a sweet gesture. It's *his* gesture. It's what he does when he wants to comfort me. If I was actually his, would he do more?

Would he be kissing me on the lips? Hugging me? Fucking me? Something else to make me forget about whatever I'm thinking?

If I said yes, I might find out.

No.

He said he wants to 'pretend marry' me. It wouldn't be any different than it was today. He would hold my hand and make polite conversations with people to make them think we are together. He would occasionally kiss my hand or kiss me on the lips. Nothing more.

But I would *get* to kiss him. And that alone would be worth the heartache of when this ended. Because this would end. Someone would find out. Or we wouldn't need each other any more.

Kade is a guy. He won't become emotionally attached, especially if there is no sex. He will use me to further his own goals, that's it.

But every brush of his lips against mine, every grin, every kind word, every touch of his hand will make me fall for him a little more until I'm completely in love with him. And then, I'll want this to be real.

Kade King is a gentleman. In fact, he's incredible. Other than the first night when he was trying to convince me to leave. That night, he was an ass. He wanted to fuck me, and we both knew it. And instead of admitting it, he treated me like dirt.

"You hungry?" Kade asks, as the car stops.

My eyes widen as I stare out the window. We're in the valet line of one of the most expensive steakhouses in town. I've never eaten here since it's not in my price range, but I'm drooling thinking about the food I've seen from Sebastian and his friends' Instagram posts of this place.

My stomach growls.

Kade laughs. "I'll take that as a yes."

I wince and nod.

He releases my hand, runs his hand through his hair, and jumps out to beat the valet to my door.

I stare at him wide-eyed, still not speaking, as he smirks. He picks my hand up off my lap, helping me stand. My ankle throbs as I stand, but I'm not going to let it ruin whatever is happening.

Kade is pretending to be my date and wants to fake marry me. That is all my brain can process at the moment.

I take a step, and my heel catches in the cobblestone.

Kade's prepared and tightens his grip on my arm.

"Sorry, I should have taken you home first so you could at least change shoes, but I couldn't resist bringing you here when you look this gorgeous in the dress."

I blush. He's making it harder for me to speak instead of easier.

We make it into the restaurant, only because Kade is holding me up.

"Mr. King!" the surprised hostess exclaims. "I'm so sorry if you made a reservation, it must have gotten lost. Give me one minute, and I'll make sure we have a table for you." She winks at Kade.

I grip his arm until I'm sure my nails are digging into his flesh and give her my best glare.

Kade chuckles and leans down to kiss me on the cheek.

"I think my arrangement is going to work out fantastically, but if you keep gripping my arm this hard, I won't be able to marry you because people will think you abuse me," he says.

I release my claws, but I still hold onto him, leaning harder into his chest. I can't believe this woman has the balls to flirt with Kade. She's the hostess. What happened to professionalism?

"We have a private table near the window overlooking the lake. I know it's not your usual table, but I think you will enjoy the new view," the hostess says.

I tense.

Kade nods and then leans into my ear again, causing shivers to roll through me. "Don't worry. I've never brought a date here."

I raise my eyebrow, not believing him as we follow the hostess.

"I haven't. I only bring business associates here. I can impress a date without bringing her here."

"Then, why am I here?"

He smiles. "I'm glad you haven't completely lost your voice. Because this is a mix of business and pleasure. And besides, you aren't like most woman. I need more than a fancy restaurant, fast car, and charm to convince you. You're too smart to fall for one of them alone. I need a mix of everything to win you over."

I blush again, liking his answer.

We keep walking, and every time we pass a table, the entire table stops their conversation to look up at us. For the first time in my life, I feel like I belong. These people don't know who I am, and they aren't judging me because Kade King is on my arm. My dress would win in any fight against any of the dresses in here on those who-wore-it-best shows. And I have a flashy ring, double the size of most in here, on my finger.

It feels strange, fitting into a crowd I've spent my whole life on the outskirts of. Not willingly trying to enter their world, but hating that I was never invited in.

Kade pulls out my chair, and I take a seat in the dark black chair, set in front of a white tablecloth with red flowers in the center. I turn my attention out the window, where strings of lights hang over the balcony, before the lake surrounded by flowers, fountains, and views. I didn't even know a lake existed back here, but it might be the most romantic spot in all of Santa Barbara.

Kade leans back in his chair, smirking like he thinks I'm going to be able to fix whatever problems he has.

I swallow. I can't even fix my problems. And I doubt fake marrying Kade will be the solution, however appealing it is.

A waiter appears and pours us both a glass of red wine. He also gives us a dish of bread with *butter*. I haven't had white bread with butter in ages. I only put healthy food into my body, but tonight, I'm eating anything placed in front of me.

"How did the waiter know we wanted red wine?" I ask.

Kade lifts the oversized wine glass out to me. I pick up my glass. It's so light. It must be real crystal.

"Because it's his job to know. I've come to this restaurant many times. He knows my preferences. And if either of us isn't happy with the wine, he will bring us a new glass of something else. He knows I prefer not to be disturbed or asked too many questions, so he won't, unless I let him know there is a problem."

"Oh."

"Now, to a night that will change both of our lives forever."

We clink our glasses together, and I taste the wine. It's good. I won't be asking to return my wine.

Kade watches me as I take another sip before I put the glass down. I need to drink slowly, I've already had more alcohol than I usually drink and I need a clear head if I'm going to make the correct decision.

I take a piece of bread and spread it with the butter before taking a bite.

I moan as the rich honey butter coats my tongue and slowly slips down my throat.

Kade cocks his head to the side.

"What?"

He shakes his head. "You're just sexy as hell when you do that."

I blush and put the piece of bread back on the plate.

"So tell me why you've decided we should get fake married. Because my theory is you're high or drunk."

He doesn't blink or react to my joke. He takes his piece of the bread and butters it before chomping down on it, making me wait. I hate waiting.

I raise an eyebrow.

Kade leans forward like he's about to tell me a secret.

"Because you need me."

I fold my arms and lean back with a sigh. "I don't need you or anyone else."

"Maybe. Or maybe you need *exactly* this."

I stop breathing, as I look into his dreamy eyes and cocky grin. He's going to win this. I need to make sure the terms are what I want. If not, I'm going to end up hurt.

"And why do I need this?" I ask, not looking at him, and instead, eating more of the crunchy bread that tastes like cake in my mouth.

"Because you need everything I'm offering. Money, a

place to live, a job, and a way to prove that not only can you fit into the world your family lives in, but you can rule it. You can be the top of the top. You won't have to worry about your father, mother, sister, or anyone in this town, ever looking down on you again."

I bite my lip trying to think about his words before responding, but I have too much on my mind to be patient with words.

"I don't want—"

"I need your help too," he says, cutting me off.

I giggle. "How can I help you? You're a god in this town. I couldn't possibly help a man like you."

He leans back in his chair, as he waves over a female waiter.

"Hello, Mr. King. What can I do for you?" the woman says seductively while touching his forearm.

Kade doesn't smile back at her. He ignores her and instead narrows his eyes as he looks at me like he's undressing me.

I shift uncomfortably in my seat. I turn my attention away from Kade to the woman I hate. She doesn't get to touch him like that. I glare at her.

"This is Larkyn Day," Kade says, turning the waitress' attention toward me.

I snarl at her, and the woman hesitantly removes her hand from Kade's arm.

Better.

"She's going to be my wife. We got engaged this afternoon," Kade finishes.

"Congratulations," the woman says, taking a step away from Kade. "I'll make sure the manager knows, and he'll bring some complimentary champagne and dessert to help you celebrate."

"Thank you, Theresa," Kade says.

The woman practically runs off, like she can't get away from us fast enough.

"That is how you can help me."

I frown.

"I don't understand."

"Women hit on me constantly."

I snort. "And that's a problem?"

He growls in a throaty way. "Yes, it's a problem. I don't mind casual sex, but I'm not looking for a wife or heir. Every woman I date, especially the women in this town, are looking for a proposal the second I slip my dick inside them. They want my money and prestige that would come with getting my last name."

I blush when he says the word dick, which he positively notices because the edge of his lips curl up as he says the word.

"And I will help your problem how? You'll be fake married to me, the one thing you don't want."

"Exactly, I'll be married to you. A woman who can make women run away with just a look."

I huff. "That waiter did not run away because I looked at her."

He folds his arms across his chest and gives me an oh really look.

"She ran away because you said we were engaged," I say.

"Exactly, the combination of your scowl and the ring on your finger will keep the women away. I won't have to worry about fending off women because you'll do it for me."

"I think you're missing one essential part."

His eyes deepen. "And what's that?"

"That you won't be able to do the sleeping with any of

these women part. I'll be fending off women, so I won't allow you to be married to me and fuck other women on the side. And if anyone in my family found out, it would defeat the purpose of me doing this."

He takes another bite of his bread, chewing, as a smirk forms. "Don't worry, I won't be fucking other women."

I swallow. I don't ask the follow up to my question, which is, does he plan on fucking me?

No. He can't be. He doesn't think of me in that way, and I'm far too inexperienced to be worth his time.

"So how would you see this working?" I ask.

"I'll have my lawyer write up all the details, so we don't have to worry about either of us getting hurt. But I'm thinking, stay married for one year. We would need to have a real wedding, and soon, for this to work. You could live with me. You can also work for my company if you want. And I'll pay you well for your time."

"Payment?" I ask, not sure why I didn't expect to get paid for this.

"Of course. If you were my real wife and we got divorced, you would earn half of my money. I think you deserve to be compensated well for helping me with my problem while I'm in town."

"And why do you need to be in town?" I ask.

His smile drops and I realize exactly why. Sebastian.

"Nevermind," I say.

"I'm thinking one million for one year of being married. If we decide to stay married longer than a year, we can renegotiate if our relationship still benefits us. We can..."

Kade continues rambling on and on, but I don't hear his words. All I hear is one million dollars. That would mean I could start any business I wanted. I would have earned the money.

No.

I couldn't use the money. At least, not for what I want.

I could get my family off my back.

I could have a place to live while I saved my own money to start my own business.

And I could spend it all while getting to kiss Kade anytime we were in public together.

It wouldn't be that bad.

I want to answer yes, but my heart still isn't sure I can survive this.

Especially when he grins like he knows everything I'm thinking. I need to find a way to make him grumpy, so my heart stops skipping every time he smiles.

"Do you have any terms you would like to add?" he asks.

"We would live mostly separate lives. No questions about where we come and go, or anything personal the other doesn't want to answer."

He nods.

"We only have to attend a maximum of two events for the other person a month, and it needs to be scheduled at least a week in advance."

He thinks for a minute. "Two should usually work, but exceptions may need to be made as long as it doesn't interfere with the other person's personal life."

"We don't sleep with anyone else or cheat on each other."

He smirks. "I thought I already made it clear that wouldn't be a problem."

I nod, trying to rack my brain for more.

Steaks are placed in front of us, and we both dig in, starving after not getting to eat much at my parents' party.

"I'll have my lawyer start writing everything we've

discussed in a contract, but text or call me any time if you think of anything else that needs to be added. I'll also make sure my lawyer includes a way to amend the contract in a month, so if something we didn't anticipate having to deal with arises, we can add it to the contract."

I nod, unable to answer as I chew my last bite of food.

Kade reaches across the table and grabs my hand. "You don't need to decide now. We will both think about it, and I'll have a meeting scheduled for us with my lawyer at the end of the week. You can decide then. In the meantime, we can pretend to be engaged."

I smile, enjoying pretending to be engaged already.

"Now as my fiancée, would you like to stay and have champagne and dessert, or would you like to do something else, like a movie?"

My stomach is stuffed, and I'm tired of living in his world. I need something relaxed to make sure I can at least tolerate his choice in movies.

"Movie."

He grins. "Good choice."

He grabs my hand and helps me up from the table.

"Don't you have to pay first?" I ask.

He places his hand on my waist as he leads me out. "No, I have a tab."

We slip through the restaurant and into his car and drive to the movie theater in silence, as his hand squeezes mine gently.

"I know I said this at the restaurant already, but I'm sorry I didn't stop by your place first so you could at least put on flat shoes," he says, as we walk into the theater.

"No way. I've never worn a dress this fancy, and I don't care if we are going to see a movie, I'm not changing out of it until tonight. I'm not a dress person usually, but then again, I've never worn a thousand dollar dress."

"Nine thousand, actually," he says, smirking.

I stare down at the white dress. I'm afraid I'm going to get butter on it when he orders popcorn.

We head into the dark theater to watch a romantic comedy, to my surprise. Kade is probably just trying to give me what he thinks I want, to convince me to fake marry him.

"Are you wanting to return the dress after this? Because I'm afraid I'm going to get butter all over it."

He eyes the dress and chuckles. "Even if I wanted to return it, I would have to pry it out of your hands, which would be impossible. But don't worry, you'll have plenty of more opportunities to wear more nice dresses."

I smile and pop a piece of popcorn into my mouth as he drapes his arm around the back of my shoulders. It feels incredibly normal. I lean back against his arm with ease.

I moan softly, as I pop a piece of popcorn into my mouth. It has been years since I've eaten popcorn. It's not on my healthy diet.

"Fuck it," I hear Kade say, just before his lips crash down on mine in a kiss.

I close my eyes, kissing him back as the bag of popcorn drops from my hands onto the floor. His tongue slips into my mouth, whisking me away to another world. When he pulls away, he's panting hard staring into my eyes.

"What was that for?" I ask, assuming someone is nearby he wants to make jealous. But it's so dark in here I doubt that.

He smirks. "Because I wanted to."

I bite my lip.

"How are you going to survive a year without sex?" I ask. He's a sexual man, used to getting sex regularly.

He tucks a strand of hair behind my ear as I freeze.

"You didn't listen to a word I said after I said one million, did you?"

"I caught some of it." I wince.

He shakes his head. "I'll make sure the lawyer sends the paperwork tomorrow, so you have plenty of time to read everything and decide."

I nod.

He smiles.

"But to answer your question." He leans down, so his lips brush against my ear. "I plan on fucking you any chance you'll give me."

I'm mush. My muscles don't work. My voice has closed up. I'm not even sure if my heart is beating in my chest. He just rocked my world with one sentence.

My eyes meet his, trying to understand him.

"I've wanted to fuck you since the moment I saw you in my brother's room. I just didn't think it was the best idea to fuck you that night. You were drunk, clearly inexperienced, and you were my brother's date."

I nod.

"I know you are inexperienced, and probably used to taking things slow. So that's what I plan on doing. Getting to know each other better. Go on dates. And when you're ready, I'll fuck you like you've never been fucked before."

I swallow. "I've never been fucked before."

His eyes deepen, along with his voice. "I know."

Cocky bastard.

"As I said, we can take as long as you want. Or no time at all, but I want you Larkyn. And I plan on getting what I want. So if you agree to fake marry me, know that I also plan on seducing you."

I lick my lip. *How could I be so lucky to get everything I've ever wanted?* I can lose my virginity to the sexiest man in town, who also happens to be the most caring man in town. I get one million dollars and the guarantee that Kade will fuck only me for a year. It's the kind of deal women dream about getting.

My eyes sparkle as I look at him.

"Sorry about the popcorn. I can get you another one," Kade says, still being the gentleman that he is. But I know he can be a bad boy when he wants to. And that's the version of him I want tonight.

"No, I don't want popcorn. I don't want to watch the movie either."

"No? What do you want then?"

"I want you to fuck me, and convince me to fake marry you, if for no other reason than I get your cock any night I want."

8 KADE

LARKYN WANTS me to fuck her.

I thought I would need to convince her over weeks or months. She's the type of woman that needs persuading. Not because she's a prude, but because she's been hurt before. I don't know Larkyn well, but I can feel the damage she carries around with her. She has an unhealthy relationship with her family. I'm guessing she has a reason not to trust men in her life.

But she's choosing me.

She wants me to be her first. A second ago, it was all I wanted. When I kissed her, it took everything in my body not to pull her into the closest bathroom, hike up her dress, and fuck her against a bathroom stall.

I've never wanted a woman so badly.

Larkyn's different. She doesn't want me for my money. She took the time to get to know something about me before wanting me to fuck her. She's not after my millions; I will have to practically force her to take the money that she would get if she married me.

But right now, I wish I'd just gotten a hotel near the

movie theater. It would have been faster. Instead, I'm driving her the fifteen minutes to my house.

Stupid, stupid, stupid.

She giggles as I run another red light. "You'd think you were the one who hasn't had sex before."

I growl, which makes her smile fuller.

God, I love her smiling. She only seems to do it around me. When she was with her family, she did nothing but frown. She should say yes to pretend marry me, if for no other reason than she might smile more.

"How long has it been?" she asks, beaming at me, and I know she's teasing.

"Not as long as it's been for you."

She bites her lip and kicks off her heels, putting them up on the dashboard. Usually, that would drive me mad, to have her dirty feet on my pristine dash. But with Larkyn, I want her comfortable. I thought she might be a wreck about having sex with me. But she's at ease. The second her begging words left her mouth, the panic evaporated, and a calm overtook her.

I kiss her hand again, wishing I could be kissing her more. But I don't want to make her nervous of my driving. She's been through too much already.

"It's been three or four months," I finally answer her question. I usually would never tell a woman something so personal, but she deserves to know. She opened up to me about being a virgin, even though I had guessed as much.

Her jaw drops open, and her eyes light up. "No way! I call bullshit. The great Kade King has had sex in the last three months. I bet you've had sex this week."

I shake my head. "Nope, last time was when I was home over Christmas visiting my brother. I made a mistake with Harlow. I haven't wanted a woman since."

She puffs out her lips in a huff. Her eyes cut to me, as she folds her arms across her chest.

"I'm telling the truth," I say, taking my eyes off the road for a second to see her annoyed expression.

"I know. I just can't believe I have to take back everything bad I ever thought about you."

I laugh, grab her hand, and kiss it again. I've never kissed a woman's hand before, but I can't stop doing it with Larkyn since it is the only place I can touch her right now without risking crashing.

"Be honest; you didn't think that many bad things about me, did you?"

"No, but each time you shatter my preconceptions about you it makes it that much harder to..." she stops.

"Oh, hell no. You aren't getting off that easy. You finish that sentence."

"And, if I don't?"

"Then, no sex."

She chuckles, and her eyes deepen as she realizes I'm telling the truth.

"You're serious? You wouldn't have sex with me if I didn't finish that sentence?"

"Yep. I've been through plenty of droughts before. I can hold out until you tell me."

She stares at my dick, which is giving me away by pressing against the zipper of my pants.

"I doubt that," she chuckles. "But fine. I'll answer. I'm afraid I'm going to fall in love with you if we do this."

I frown, my head snapping to her. "If we have sex?"

"Not sex. If we pretend marry. Live together. Are friends. Continue to have sex. All of it. I'm afraid I'll fall in love with you, and you won't feel the same. I'll get hurt."

Fuck, that's a lot to take in.

Her eyes widen when I pull through the gate.

"This is your house?" she asks, her body leaning forward so she can get a better view out the window.

"Yes, I prefer condos. I have a condo in LA and New York, but I thought I should own at least one house. Makes me feel more like a grownup. Besides, there aren't any nice condos nearby."

As we pull up to the door, we both undo our seatbelts and stare up at my modern mansion. I thought if I designed it as modern as possible, it would feel more like a condo instead of a house. It would feel more like mine. Instead, all it feels is cold.

I open my door and go around to open hers, still thinking about what she said. I can understand why she might think that, but it's not something she should worry about. No one ever falls in love with me. Not after they get to know me. I'm putting on the charm now because I like her and want something from her. But as soon as that changes, I'll be an ass. She'll figure it out soon enough.

I help her out of the car onto her bare feet, her heels dangling in her hands. I pull her against my body roughly. Her breath catches, and her body stiffens against mine.

"I'll hurt you long before you fall in love with me. We'll fight, I'll sleep in a hotel for a night or two, and then we will go back to being friends. That is how our story ends. You don't have to worry about falling in love with me. You were right. I'm a cocky asshole."

She smiles, but her eyes don't believe me.

I sigh. She's about to find out how much of a bad boy I can be. I should back off. Let her think about this more. Find a way to protect her heart. But I'm not going to do that. Instead, I'm going to move faster.

I kiss her. Her head tilts to the side as her lips part

wider, giving me more access to her tantalizing tongue. If she's half as good at sex as she is at kissing, I'm in trouble. My head is already spinning with thoughts of her. If fucking her is incredible, I won't be going to work for days.

Her tiny body is pressed against mine as I start walking her backward, toward the entrance to my house. She winces when she takes an awkward step back.

"See, I can't even remember that you have a hurt leg? How much of an ass does that make me?" I ask.

She grins against my lips, her eyes closed. "The biggest."

I scoop her up, but instead of holding her bridal style, I throw her over my shoulder and smack her ass, making sure she's at least a little-pissed off at me for manhandling her. It will make the sex better.

"Dammit, Kade!"

I laugh as I open the door.

"Oh sorry, I thought I should try to be a gentleman, and carry you with your hurt leg and all."

"No, you aren't. You're a jerk. You could carry me sweetly. Stop trying to be an ass and just be yourself."

"This is me, baby. Get used to it."

I storm through my house, upstairs to my bedroom, and toss her onto my bed. She falls in a huff. Her white, lace dress covers most of my dark blue comforter.

She looks like heaven, and she's about to find out how much of a devil I can be.

She's smiling behind her glare. She's pretending to be mad at me, just like I'm pretending to drive her crazy so she won't fall for me. Not that she would on the first night anyway.

Larkyn glances around, taking in the large room with floor to ceiling windows looking out to the woods behind my house.

"Why don't you have blinds?" she asks, trying to see if anyone can peer into my bedroom.

I take my time removing my jacket, tie, and shirt.

She finally looks my way, and her body blushes red at the sight of my bare chest. She bites her lip as she examines the tattoos on my chest. She rapidly blinks, like she can't believe what her eyes are seeing.

"Never seen a shirtless man before?" I tease.

She grabs the single throw pillow on my bed, and tosses it at me, but misses.

"Of course I have. The tattoos caught me off guard. Maybe you're the bad boy I originally thought you were."

I kick off my shoes and lower my pants and boxer briefs in one push.

"Maybe I am," I say, winking at her. Her eyes try desperately to stay on my chest instead of looking at my throbbing cock, which grows larger every second she stares at me with those big eyes of hers.

"It's okay, you can look," I say, walking toward her.

She swallows. "Um..."

Speechless, perfect. This is going to be fun, torturing her.

She finally takes a peek, and her hand covers her mouth to hold in her gasp. Her eyes are almost popping out of her head, and her cheeks are red.

I laugh. "First time seeing a cock?"

"No, just...um...yours is...um."

"You like it?"

"Yes," she breathes, finally gaining the confidence to look me in the eyes. And when she does, everything disappears. The embarrassment. The playfulness. The tinge of anger.

It's all replaced with lust.

She wants to fuck me. She's desperate for it. *Good.*

I pull open the drawer and find a condom, tossing it on the bed, so I don't have to find one later.

She bites her lip and runs her hands over my abs.

"I like these," she says.

I grin.

I flip her over and am rewarded with a whimper.

I unzip and pull off her dress sharply, before flipping her back over to get my own glimpse of her abs.

"I like these," I growl in return, before lowering my head to kiss her smooth stomach, rippling with muscles.

She grins and runs her hands through my hair, as I work my way up her body. Kissing over her white bra and cleavage, to her neck, and finally finding her mouth.

So many whimpers escape her lips, and this time her cheeks flush with need instead of embarrassment.

She arches her back as I kiss her, forcing my cock into her stomach. I swear I almost come like a fifteen-year-old boy from the touch of her body against mine.

What's wrong with me?

I need to slow this down if I want a chance at making her come on my cock and not embarrass myself. It's just because it's been so long without sex. That's all. It has nothing to do with the particular woman underneath me.

"How could a woman as beautiful and intelligent as you still be a virgin?" I ask, as I slow my kisses on her neck.

The question was meant to be rhetorical. It was meant to be a compliment, but from the way her body has stilled, I don't think she took it that way.

I stop, leaning off her body.

"I didn't mean anything by it. I just meant you are so incredible. I can't believe how lucky I am that I get to be with you first. I'm amazing in bed, so you're pretty lucky that you get to learn from the best," I say, with a wink.

She doesn't smile. She doesn't move.

"I should tell you before we do this," she says, sitting up, pushing my naked body back.

I narrow my eyes at her, not understanding her words.

"I don't want you to find out later, think I was hiding it, and it ruin our friendship," she says.

I tuck a strand of her hair behind her ear, but it does nothing to tame the wildness of her hair that already looks like I fucked her.

"There is nothing you could tell me that will make me stop wanting to fuck you right now."

She takes a deep breath before looking at me in the same way. And if she keeps staring at me like she is now, she won't have time to say anything.

"Then tell me. Because I can't wait any longer to fuck you."

She bites her lip, and this looks like it's going to be a long conversation.

"Actually, lay back," I say.

"Why?" She raises an eyebrow.

I sigh. "Will you just do what I say?"

"No."

I shake my head. "You trust me to be your first, but not to give you a simple command?"

She blushes.

I grab her legs, spreading them on either side of my body as I pull her roughly until she's lying on her back. Then, my face buries between her legs.

She gasps when I kiss over her panties to her most sensitive area.

"I can't talk if you keep doing that," she says, arching her back as I pull her panties down.

"What if I do this?"

I lick my tongue slowly over her slit, then up to her bud, swollen and ready for me.

She gasps again, gripping my bedspread.

"You need to stop."

I lick again, and her legs clasp against my head. There is no way I'm stopping.

"Has anyone licked you before, Larkyn?" I ask.

"No," she moans, as I continue.

"Good. Then, I get the pleasure of tasting you as you come on my face for the first time."

"Don't stop," she pants when I slow my tongue again.

I grin and speed up my pace. Not relenting or letting her get a second to think about whatever has her worried that I won't want to do this with her.

Her body tightens, her eyes roll back, and her hands grasp the comforter so forcefully, I think she might rip a hole in it.

"Come, Larkyn," I whisper against her pussy as I continue torturing her with my mouth.

Her legs lock my head in a headlock, she cries out, and her lips grip my tongue as her orgasm rips through her.

I lick every drop of cum off her body, letting her know how much I enjoyed that, and how much more I'm going to enjoy fucking her and making her come again with my cock.

I move up her body while she pants on the bed, exhausted and alive after the pleasure I brought her.

I smirk as I pop her bra open, and let my mouth come down on one of her sensitive nipples.

"Kade, I can't again—"

I silence her with a flick of my tongue on her nipple, and she's mine again.

She claws at my back as I continue my assault on her body, finding every sensitive area I can and exploiting it. Making it *mine*.

Her breasts, neck, and just above her hip are all sensitive areas I'll have to remember for the future.

"You still with me?" I ask, nerves slipping in as I reach for the condom.

She swallows hard, as her eyes lazily drop to my cock. I want her mouth on my dick, but that will have to wait until later. Right now, I need to make her feel even more incredible than she did with her last orgasm.

She nods, answering my question.

"Good, because I'm about to rock your world."

"That's cheesy," she says with a grin, as my lips come down and kiss her.

When I pull back, I tear the condom open with my teeth and sheath myself with it before resting between her legs.

Her breathing slows, and I feel the slickness escaping her, trying to welcome me in.

I need her permission. One more time first. And now I'm nervous. Why? Because I don't want to screw this up. Whatever this is between us, I like it. I like helping her, and I think she would like helping me.

Sex changes things. But it won't change us.

I don't ask her again with words. Instead, I press my cock at her entrance as I kiss her. Giving her a warning that if she doesn't stop me, she's mine. And I'm hers. I'll be her first.

"I'm not a virgin," she whispers.

I stop, but my dick doesn't soften. I don't give a fuck if she's a virgin or not.

"Doesn't matter."

"I was raped at nineteen, that's why I'm technically not," she says.

I suck in a breath, searching in her eyes for the pain. It's there, but tampered. She hasn't thought about that night for a long time.

"You're a virgin, then," I say, letting her know that whatever that asshole did to her doesn't mean he took her virginity.

I'm taking it.

She smiles. "I've waited a long time to find the perfect guy to be my first."

I smirk. "I'm pretty perfect, aren't I?"

She gives me a wicked stare. "Too perfect."

I kiss her lips. I'll stop and spend the rest of the night listening to her story.

"You can tell me every detail of how the guy raped you. I can be that guy for you. Or I can be the guy who fucks you and destroys his memory in your mind. Makes it all but disappear. No longer mattering. I know he's practically gone anyway because you aren't broken. You're strong. So which guy do you want me to be?" I know what guy I want to be, but she has to choose.

She looks away, and I'm afraid she's going to choose the talking route. After all of this, she's going to be the woman I thought she was all along. Cautious. Thinking with her brain, instead of her heart.

"Be the guy that fucks my brains out, and makes me an insatiable sex addict," she says, with a wicked glance.

"My pleasure." My cock slides into her with ease, her slick entrance coating me as I push inside.

My eyes stay on her, even as my lips kiss her, looking for any signs that this too much for her. That I'm bringing back nightmares or thoughts of him. I will be asking more questions later because I want to make sure the bastard is in prison. No one gets to hurt Larkyn Day ever again.

Her eyes stay open too.

"Incredible," she says, smiling.

I realize that I'm not moving. I'm frozen except for my lips kissing hers. I've been too afraid that I will physically or emotionally hurt her if I move.

"That's what I was thinking about you," I say, as I start to rock in out of her body. Treasuring every bit of her body as I do.

Her moans.

Her grin.

Her gaze.

Her body is holding onto me like she will never let me go.

I feel her building the faster I move, so I move faster and faster. I cradle her body tenderly in my arms while fucking her like no woman I have before.

I don't have to say a word. She doesn't either. We look at each other, and we come, together.

Both of our orgasms shoot through us like a fire that can't be contained.

I collapse next to her on the bed. I'm spent. I only fucked her once. Usually, I fuck a woman at least twice, but fucking Larkyn is like fucking a million women at once. Better actually, because Larkyn is the only woman I've fucked who is only interested in my dick and me. Nothing else. Not my money, my fancy cars, or my expensive condos. She doesn't want a baby to make me hers. She doesn't even want a real marriage. This isn't a trap. It's just her and me, fucking.

Larkyn begins to move off the bed, but I grab her hips and force her down, my body her trapping her.

"Where are you going?"

"Home, I didn't think you would enjoy having a woman sleep with you in your bed. Even one you might be fake marrying soon."

I frown. Usually, I would hate women that think they are going to sleep over after sex. But the fact that Larkyn didn't assume she was staying makes me like her even more.

"You're staying."

"What?" Her eyes blink rapidly.

"I want you here in my bed. If I fuck you, you're staying. You don't get to slink out in the night."

She narrows her eyes studying me.

"Even if I was living with you?"

"If I fuck you, you're mine for the night. You don't get to sleep alone." I want to add ever to the end of my sentence but don't. I want her in my bed for the entire year. So I can have my way with her whenever I want, but I think it might be too much to ask of her.

I roll off her and pull her to me as I pull the covers over our naked bodies. Her body fits snuggly in the crook of mine. Her head rests against my arm, and she's so small I doubt my arm will ever tire of having her lay on it all night.

"Yes," she says.

"What?" I ask, rolling her over to look at me.

"I'll fake marry you," she says grinning.

Yes, such a beautiful word.

"Good. Now get some sleep, so you have enough strength for me to fuck you in the morning."

She giggles as I wrap my arms around her again. "I have another condition though."

"Which is?"

"I want you to get me a smaller ring."

I laugh.

"Or a fake one to replace this one. I can't wear this expensive of a ring."

I kiss her on the lips. "No, you deserve the best."

The absolute best. She deserves everything. And I plan on giving her everything. I have to remember that it's okay to be an ass, too. Because there is no way, I'm letting her fall in love with me and ruin us. And I couldn't live with myself if I hurt her.

9 LARKYN

IT'S BEEN a week since I slept with Kade.

It's what I wanted. A week apart after he rocked my world and made me realize what I've been missing all these years. I regret not having sex sooner if it is always that amazing. I'm afraid it might only be *that* incredible with Kade, and not any of other guys.

Kade has, mostly, respected my wishes to stay away. Only because I told him I needed to study for my final exams. I didn't need to study. I have straight A's and could have failed every one of my tests and still graduated. But Kade didn't know that. So he stayed away, except for a few naughty text messages telling me how much he missed my body.

I glance up at the stage where some rich man is speaking, trying to be inspirational. Saying things about how we are the future, and graduating from a prestigious school like this means we can do anything. It's the usual words. Nothing will make a difference in any of our lives. Thousands of students sit in chairs next to me, all waiting for him to finish talking so we can throw our graduation caps in the air and celebrate.

Only problem is, I don't have any family here to celebrate with. I texted my father on Thursday when it was official that I was graduating on Friday. He texted back that he had a meeting in Chicago and couldn't be here. My mother is too drunk to come. And Anastasia won't attend anything that isn't all about her, especially after I overshadowed her engagement with my own.

I stare down at my bare finger. I chose not to wear the ring today. Today is about me.

My family isn't here.

Kade isn't here.

Today, I'm on my own.

The man finally stops talking, and we throw our caps up in the air. We are graduates now. But I find myself wondering why I bothered attending the ceremony. I should have just stayed home to packed and had the school mail me my diploma. And I should have texted Kade to hang out instead. I need to text him so we can talk about the documents his lawyer sent over earlier this week.

I catch my cap as it falls. My immediate thought is to text Kade to see if he's busy tonight so we can talk, and do other things... I bite my lip as my mind is clouded with thoughts of having sex with Kade again.

But I know Serena is going to want me to hang out with her and her family to celebrate graduating. And then I should really start packing. We have to be out of our apartment in a week.

I start walking across the auditorium floor to the other side, where I know Serena was sitting, to meet her.

"Beautiful and intelligent, how lucky am I?" I hear Kade say from behind me.

I grin. I've never smiled so much in my life as I have the few days I've spent with Kade.

I turn around. "And why are you lucky?"

He holds out the most massive bouquet of flowers in the auditorium to me. I take it from him, barely able to wrap my hands around the stems.

"Because I get to spend the next year with you."

I try to hide my smile, but it's impossible. "And why do you think that? I haven't officially signed any papers yet."

"You already said yes. Twice," he winks as he says twice, and I know he's referring to me coming twice the last time we were together.

I reach into my oversized purse that is draped over my shoulder and hand him the papers I signed last night.

He grins like an idiot, as he takes the papers from me and flips to the last page with my signature. He takes a pen from his pocket and signs it as well.

"Now it's official. You're mine for the year."

My hands tremble a little at that thought. I want nothing more than to be his. I just need to remind my body that despite his words and actions, I'm not his.

He glances down at my hand. "Why aren't you wearing your ring?"

I sigh.

"Because I wanted one last day where I belonged to myself, and not to you."

He frowns and pulls the ring out of his pocket. He grabs my hand and places it into my hand.

"For when you're ready to be mine," he says.

I stare at the ring in the palm of my hand. Take a deep breath. And slip the heavy diamond onto my finger. I signed the papers. We are getting married next weekend. I might as well get used to wearing the enormous rock. I don't know how he has the ring. Did Serena let him in?

He smiles, and the smile is almost worth the cost of having to wear something so flashy.

"Where is your family? Are we headed to another graduation party?" he asks, as he drapes his arm over my shoulders and looks around to find my family.

"They aren't here."

He narrows his eyes, searching mine for answers.

"I'm sorry."

"It doesn't matter. My family doesn't matter. But I wouldn't expect them to attend the wedding either. They want nothing to do with me unless I do as I'm told."

He hugs me tight against his chest as the flowers rest by my side so my face can sink into his body. I take a deep breath and smell his deep cologne. It shouldn't comfort me, but it does.

"Oh my god! Are you two together?" Serena squeals, looking from Kade down to me.

I try to step out of his arms, but he holds me tight. He's always touching me or holding me. Something I'm afraid I'll get used to far too quickly.

I nod and blush.

"Getting married, actually," Kade says.

Serena's mouth drops, along with the diploma and graduation cap she was holding. She glances down and quickly picks it up again.

"You can't be serious? I didn't even know you were... I mean, when did this happen?" Serena asks, flustered and staring right at me. I know she's annoyed that I have been hiding Kade and I's relationship from her.

I wince. "It's a long story."

"A story you will be giving me every detail of later."

I nod.

"Good."

Serena looks behind her where her family is waiting for her.

"So I'm guessing you're a no then for celebrating with my family and me?" Serena asks with a smug expression on her face as she crosses her arms.

I nod, biting my lip.

She shakes her head and runs over to hug me. Kade drops his arm from my shoulders as she wraps her arms around me.

"I mean *every* detail later," Serena says, winking.

"Don't worry, I'll tell you everything. You're my maid of honor after all."

Her face lights up, and her grin reaches her eyes. "Damn right, I am," she says, as she struts away.

"We should celebrate. What is your favorite restaurant?" Kade asks.

"I don't eat out much. I don't have a favorite restaurant."

Kade sighs as he stands next to me, staring, as people continue walking by us. Every person that walks by stares at Kade and then to me with wide-eyes or a glare. They don't believe we belong together. And we don't.

"I have the perfect seafood restaurant to try. Do you like sushi?"

I stare down at the flowers and diploma I'm still holding. I'm supposed to go to a restaurant to celebrate with family and friends. Except my family is a no-show, and I just turned down my best friend. And I'm marrying a man that I've slept with once, and might as well be a complete stranger.

"I have a better idea," I reach up, grab his neck, and kiss him on the lips, slipping my tongue into his mouth. Our bodies collide, and I drop the flowers, along with my diploma to the ground.

He's not really mine. He's not really mine. He's not really mine.

But when he grabs my face and deepens the kiss, moaning into my mouth, I forget that he's not mine.

"I like your idea better; food can wait until after. Your place or mine?"

I grin.

"Mine's closer."

———

I OPEN the door to my apartment with Kade's lips locked on mine when my leg hits a box that shouldn't be sitting in the entryway.

I pause the kiss and stare into my apartment. Boxes are everywhere. Boxes that weren't here when I left this morning.

"What?" I can't speak because I don't even know what questions to ask.

I turn to Kade who has a smirk on his face. "*You*. What did you do?"

"I hired movers to box everything up. Your lease ends in a few days, and I knew you'd say yes. So I went ahead and had them get started packing so you can move in with me ASAP."

I frown. "I'm not moving in with you until we are married."

He sighs. "I figured you'd say that. But your stuff is already packed. All of it. You can't exactly stay here."

I narrow my eyes and cross my arms. "I can and I will."

He shakes his head. "So stubborn."

I hold my ground. I may have signed the papers, but I'm not letting him think he can control me. He can't. Ever. And he certainly isn't going to start now.

"Fine. You can stay here until we get married next week."

I grin. "Thanks, but I don't need your permission."

I start walking toward the bedroom as Kade follows me. I stop abruptly and turn to Kade.

"Wait, how did you get into my apartment without me knowing? How did you get the ring back?" I ask holding up my hand.

He shrugs.

"Kade," I say sternly.

"I like you being all bossy. I got Serena's number at the hospital. It happened to come in handy."

"She knows?"

"Not all the details, like about how good I was in bed, but I'm sure you'll fill her in on that later. But yea, she knows."

Pink flushes my cheeks as I think back to Serena's reaction. "But she said..." I trail off.

Kade raises an eyebrow at me, smiling.

"Damn, she's a good actress," I mumble.

I open the door to my bedroom and gasp. My bed frame is in pieces, covered in bubble wrap, while my mattress is sandwiched between my wall and half a dozen boxes.

I pout. *Why can't I have this one thing? All I want is to have Kade fuck me in my bed to celebrate graduating from college. Why is it so hard for the universe to understand?*

I turn to Kade. "I guess we should have gone to your place."

He smirks, and his eyes darken as he walks toward me in his designer jeans and dark buttoned up shirt that reveals the hint of muscles lying beneath his shirt. I eye the growing hardness trapped in his jeans. He still wants me.

His thumb caresses my face as he kisses me again, harder than he should since we don't have a place to fuck unless we use Serena's bed. And I'm not going to deal with her wrath if she found out or came home early.

"Who says I need a bed to fuck you?"

I lick my lips, and my pussy aches as he speaks. I've had sex once. I'm not an idiot, but we don't have a bed. Or a couch. Or even a table to have sex on. I don't know what's left.

Kade grabs my hips, and we move backward until my back hits the wall behind me. He grins as his lips find mine again. Tasting and swirling around my tongue, making me lose my mind.

His hand slips under my dress, pushing it up, and finds my bare ass beneath the thong I'm wearing. His fingers hook the edge of my lace thong and pull them down until they fall to my feet. He watches them hit my ankles, and then I step out of them still wearing my heels.

"You found some prettier lingerie, huh?" he asks, as he kisses my neck.

"I didn't think you were too fond of my plain cotton panties."

He gives me a wicked grin. "They were starting to grow on me. And remind me to punish you later for wearing heels again and no brace."

His hand slips up my backside again before slapping me on the ass.

I let out a yelp.

"My doctor said I don't need to wear my braces any longer."

He eyes me suspiciously. "I doubt that."

"It's true." I kiss him on the lips and undo his pants to shut him up. I shove them down along with his boxer briefs, and immediately feel his erection in my stomach pressing hard, begging me to enter.

He spanks me again.

I gasp.

"You aren't going to be able to distract me with sex all the time you know." He steps back and pulls his shirt off until he's naked.

I bite my lip. I may not be able to, but I sure will try.

He picks up his pants and pulls out a condom. He sheaths himself with the latex before returning to kiss me hard against the wall. He shoves my dress up, grabs my ass, and I impale myself on his cock.

My hands grab onto his hair as he thrusts inside me, holding me up while fucking me against the wall. He rocks harder and harder inside me, knowing that he doesn't have to do much to make me come. My moaning gives me away; I'm very close to giving into the desires deep in my belly that are begging to explode out.

I try to speak. But everything that comes out of my mouth is a mix of a moan, groan, and holy hell pant.

His eyes sear into mine, as our tongues dance together. He knows what he's doing to me. But I seem to be doing the same to him.

He growls, and my body tightens around his cock, I can't hold on any longer. I come, and it's like a thousand fireworks go off in my body all at once. Last time, I came because his tongue was on my clit dancing. I came a second time that night, because of how much he stirred my body from the first orgasm.

But now, he made me come with just his cock, and I never want to come without his cock again.

He doesn't lower me immediately after we both come. Nor does he remove his cock. We stay locked, holding on to every last fleeting moment of pleasure. Because even though this is only the second time we've fucked, our time together is only for a year. And our agreement doesn't mean that we have to have sex for the entire year either. Although, I plan on taking advantage of every day of our year together.

He nibbles on my lip. "I'm hungry and need a shower. Let's order food, and then shower together while we wait for the food."

"Shower together?" I ask, stupidly.

He chuckles. "I forget how inexperienced you are when you fuck me like that. But yes, I plan on fucking you every way I can, in every place I can. Shower, kitchen, bedroom, living room, public places, everywhere."

He gently lowers me down to my feet. He winks and picks up his jeans to dig out his phone.

I lean against the wall, smiling like an idiot.

"Sushi, okay?" Kade asks.

"Yes," I say, taking a step forward. But my heels don't hold me, and I fall in a heap to the floor. My injured wrist catches myself on the floor, and the sharp pain immediately reminds me that although most of the bruises have healed enough to be covered with makeup, my wrist and leg have not.

Kade is kneeling in front of me in seconds. He gently holds out his hand to me, as I hold my injured wrist tenderly.

"Let me see," he says sternly.

I hold out my wrist that is red and inflamed. He takes it in his hand eyeing it carefully with concern on his face before he kisses it carefully.

"I'll go get some ice and see if I can find any painkillers," he says.

He leaves me sitting naked on the carpet of my bedroom as he heads to the kitchen.

"This changes nothing! We are still having shower sex!" I holler after him.

I hear him chuckle. "Only if you wear your brace," he hollers back as I listen to him open the freezer and scrape out some ice.

"Fine!" I shout back. My wrist hurts, and I'll do anything for another opportunity to have sex with Kade. We are going to need some boundaries if this is how I feel after only the second time fucking. Maybe the more we do it, the less effect it will have on me.

I try moving my wrist, but it burns to move it at all, so instead, I lie it carefully on my knee. I kick off my heels that I never plan on wearing again. They are the damn reason I keep falling. I wait patiently for Kade to return.

I don't know if it's the pain in my wrist, or if Kade is really slow at getting ice that makes the time move by so slowly.

"Kade, I only need a small bag of ice. Not an iceberg large enough to sink the Titanic," I shout.

Nothing.

I sigh. *Did he just leave?*

I use my good arm to push myself up into a standing position. Fuck, my ankle hurts too. I should put some ice on it as well. I grab Kade's shirt and slip it on, before walking to the kitchen where Kade is.

He doesn't look at me when I enter.

"What are you doing?" I ask. He's standing in my kitchen holding a bag of ice.

"I need to go," he says.

He walks to me and hands me the bag of ice. Then continues back to my bedroom. I take a deep breath, trying not to be upset. We aren't dating; of course, he can go and not tell me why. He doesn't need a reason. We are a fake relationship. This isn't real. We have sex and pretend we are together. That's all this is.

But the tears threatening my eyes say I want this to be more.

Dammit.

I can't be feeling this way already. I blink back the tears and put the ice on my wrist.

Kade reappears from my bedroom moments later in his jeans. He walks over to me, and I think he's going to give me an explanation or at least say he's sorry.

"I'm going to need my shirt," Kade says.

"Oh," is all that leaves my mouth. I quickly remove the shirt until I'm standing naked in front of him, and he's fully dressed.

And then, he walks out my front door without a good-bye, a kiss on the cheek, or any words at all.

I hate him.

Good.

That's what I wanted. To know that he can live up to his bad boy reputation and be just as bad to me as everyone else. It will stop me from feeling special. And will help me remember that after the year is up, I'll return to being nothing to him.

I head to the shower. I don't want to smell like him and be reminded of him all night. So I shower and put on a shirt and sweatpants that I find at the top of one of the boxes labeled clothing. I spend a few minutes digging my bathroom items out of boxes, and then I grab the ice I left in the freezer before my shower. I head to Serena's bed to ice my ankle and wrist. I guess I'm sleeping in her bed with her for the next few nights. Good thing she has a king-sized bed.

I'll spend the night icing my sore body and watching horror movies to distract myself from being pissed at Kade for walking out without an explanation.

A knock on the door stops me in my tracks. *Did Kade decide to come back?*

I walk to the door carefully, so I don't fall and injure myself again. I open the door.

"Delivery for a Miss Day," the man says, dressed in jeans and a dark shirt.

"I'm sorry, but I didn't order anything."

He holds out the bag to me. "It's already been paid for by a Mr. King who said to tell you he is incredibly sorry and to give you this note."

I take the note and the bag from him before going back inside. I place the bag on my kitchen counter and read the note.

LARKYN,

I'm sorry I left without a goodbye or explanation. I'm not used to being accountable to another person. A family emergency came up that I need to take care of. So sorry to cut our night short. I'll make up the shower sex to you soon. Promise. Stop being stubborn and ice your ankle and wrist. And wear your braces. I'll punish you if you don't.

—Kade

.   .   .

DAMMIT.

One note and a container of sushi and I like him again. I can't even go one night without hating him. My heart doesn't stand a chance at not falling in love during this next year.

10 KADE

I'M GETTING MARRIED to the perfect woman. Not because I love her or want a normal marriage with her, but because she is exactly what I need to make my problems go away. Women will stop hitting on me and trying to trap me by getting pregnant. And after we get divorced, women will realize that Larkyn got almost nothing in the divorce. One million is nothing to these women. They will realize I'm not worth the effort. It's a brilliant plan.

Now I have to stand at the end of the aisle with Axel, my best friend, and hope Larkyn actually walks down the aisle and marries me, instead of making me look like a fool by not showing up. She's signed the contract, and the money will be deposited in her account the second she says 'I do,' but it's still a lot to ask of her.

I've barely seen Larkyn this week. The handful of times I've seen her were when we were meeting to decide which cake or flowers we were going to use. Or when we met with the overly ambitious wedding planner, I hired to get the wedding planned in less than a week at the five-star hotel I'm currently standing in. I'll give it to our wedding planner and Serena; together they made a great team and somehow came in under the budget I gave them, while giving me everything I wanted.

Larkyn didn't have an opinion about any of the details. I was afraid I was even going to have to pick out her wedding dress for her. Luckily, I didn't, so I have no idea what she is going to look like walking toward me. For all I know, she will be in jeans and a tank top.

I haven't had time to fully explain to Larkyn since I walked out on her. She's still pissed; she has a right to be. But I'll spend this week making it up to her, because I don't plan on leaving her side after we say our vows.

If I play my cards right, I'll get her to work for me as my assistant so she can go with me everywhere. I grin, liking that idea too much. I would never get any work done with her so near, driving my cock mad, stopping to fuck her every time we were alone. But I won't be getting any work done without her.

Sebastian shifts in his seat in the front row, and my grin drops. He's under strict instructions to not fuck up today. I don't know whether to thank him for running over Larkyn or to kill him. He's the reason I'm getting married right now. But he's also the reason Larkyn's pissed at me and might back out. I had to fix another one of his fucking problems the night I walked out on her, just like I always do. He's got one year to get his shit together; after that, I'm done helping him.

The music changes, and I turn my attention down the long aisle lined with flowers. The doors open, and Serena starts walking in a lavender dress. It's a good sign seeing her smiling and winking at me. Her hair is swept to the side in defined dark curls.

When she gets to me, I ask, "Is Larkyn here? How is she?"

She smiles. "Look for yourself."

I swivel my head as the main doors close, then reopen with a new song. Larkyn is standing there, on the arm of her father.

I exhale for the first time in minutes. Her father came and is walking her down the aisle. He better have after the lecture I gave him. But I don't give a damn about him right now.

All I can focus on is the goddess floating toward me. Larkyn isn't wearing a giant expensive dress. It's a simple, understated dress. Spaghetti straps hug her shoulders, lace covers the bodice, and chevron fabric hangs down from her chest. Compared to everything else in the room, she looks simple. There is no way she spent much money on the dress. But she looks even more stunning because she isn't over the top. She's just herself. Hair down and curled. No veil, only a few white flowers in her hair. And flat shoes.

I grin. At least she listened to one of my requests. I won't have to worry about her falling and injuring herself every second of the reception.

Larkyn and her father stop a foot from me. He gives me a stern look before holding out his daughter's hand to me. I take it, without giving a shit about the man who has treated his daughter like crap for the last twenty years.

"You look like an angel. So beautiful," I croak out, my voice breaking because it's so dry from gaping at her.

She blushes. "I used my own money to buy the dress. I wanted something that was mine to wear. I hope it's enough."

My eyes widen. "It's more than enough." I kiss her gently on the cheek.

"You still pissed at me?" I ask.

She licks her lips as her eyes tear through my tuxedo. "I can't stay mad at you, no matter how hard I try."

I smirk. "Good, because I really need the hot wedding sex tonight. This week has been torture for me."

She bites her lip. "Me too."

Damn, that's sexy.

"You ready?" I ask, eyeing the impatient minister out of the corner of my eye.

She smirks. "Yes."

———

WE'RE MARRIED.

I'm not sure it has sunk in yet, but the ring on my finger tells me otherwise. And the look in my bride's eyes tells me it's true.

"You got me a simple ring," Larkyn says, holding up the plain gold band I bought her to serve as her wedding ring. "Does that mean I don't have to wear the enormous engagement ring all the time?"

My lips thin a little. The engagement ring has a lot of sentimental value to me. I'd love for her to wear it always, although I know it's not realistic for her to. It's too big and doesn't fit her style. I should tell her why the ring means so much to me, and why I want her to wear it, but I'm not ready to share my story, yet.

I kiss her hand where both rings rest as we sit in the backseat of a limo on the way to my house. I thought about getting a hotel room for the night, but I don't want her in a hotel room. I want her at my house where she belongs.

"You only have to wear it to parties or events you attend with me."

She relaxes her head on my shoulder. "We need to get a safe for it when I'm not wearing it, so I don't lose it."

I kiss the top of her head. My life is perfect. Everyone believed our wedding to be real. No woman hit on me at the reception. In fact, most of the single woman tried to give me a wide berth when walking near me. Larkyn's family seemed to believe what we have is real. Her father even appeared a bit proud when he looked at Larkyn, though he will never admit it to her.

"So are you whisking me to an exotic place for our honeymoon?" she asks, yawning.

I pull her closer into me, and she cuddles her head against my chest. We have at least a thirty-minute drive from here to my house.

"No, sorry," I say chuckling.

"That's okay. I was hoping we could stay at your place. I'm too exhausted to want to travel all over the world."

I stroke her hair, loving having her head against my chest. "We will go on a belated honeymoon in the fall or around the holidays if you want. Now isn't a good time with everything going on at work." *Or with Sebastian*, I think, but don't tell Larkyn. I need to keep my thoughts of my brother private from Larkyn.

"Stressed?" she asks.

"Not as much anymore, now that we are married," I say.

Her eyes flutter open, and I can see she has a dark thought.

"What?"

She licks her lips. "I can help you relieve some stress."

Yes. God, yes.

"I think I've flipped a switch in your head and changed you from innocent to sex goddess," I say, loving the look she's giving me.

I think she's going to straddle my lap so I can fuck her in the back of the limo, but she doesn't.

Instead, her hands go for the button and zipper on my pants. She undoes my pants and slowly pushes them down, along with my underwear until my cock springs free.

She eyes me as she licks her lips again. She hesitates for a second and grasps my cock firmly with her hand. Rubbing it up and down gently.

I gasp. She has never touched my cock with her hand. Either she wasn't brave enough, or I never gave her the chance.

She grins when she sees my reaction.

"You don't ever have to ask to touch me like this," I say between heated breaths.

She keeps her gorgeous, big eyes on me as she lowers her lips and sucks the head.

My eyes roll back in my head as a curse leaves my lips at how incredible the blissful touch of her lips on me feels.

I open my eyes to watch as her mouth takes most of me in, and then slowly rakes her teeth back up my cock.

Sexy as hell.

I grip her hair, doing everything I can to not force her head back down over my cock. I want her to be in control. And she wouldn't let me take it from her right now even if I wanted to.

Her lips curl up as she sees what she's doing to me. Her head comes all the way off my cock as a drop of pre-cum coats the top. Her tongue licks across the tip, grabbing the drop of liquid off before she swallows it down.

I ache. Everywhere. *What is she doing to me?*

She smirks as if to show she knows exactly what she's doing. Suddenly her mouth comes down on my cock, until she has every bit of me in her mouth.

"Fuck," I moan, not able to hold back.

I buck underneath her mouth. She meets my thrusts and begins moving her mouth up and down, stroking me at the same speed I'm moving.

I can't breathe. I can't speak. All I can do is feel every bit of her mouth, tongue, and throat moving over me like an expert that has done this exact thing thousands of times before. I don't have to tell her what I want. She knows. She moves faster, harder when I want her to. She scrapes the tiniest bit of her teeth against my head and then swirls her tongue over the top before sucking me in again.

I growl, looking her dead in the eye, telling her I'm about to come, so stop sucking me if she doesn't want to taste my cum. I can't speak, so it's the only way I can warn her.

She grins around my cock and takes me in further as I shoot my load down her throat. My cock pulses over and over in her mouth, until she's milked every last drop from me.

When I finish, she neatly tucks me back into my pants with the broadest smile possible on her face.

"You've done that before," I say, watching her smirk.

"No."

"Then, how?"

She blushes.

"How?" I ask again.

"I did a few internet searches..." She winces and blushes like it's a bad thing.

I chuckle. "You watched porn?"

She nods.

I laugh, a full belly laugh. I grab her steaming red cheeks and kiss her on the lips. "You're incredible. Don't ever be ashamed of watching porn. I kind of like it."

She leans back like she's exhausted.

"Oh, you don't get to be tired yet."

"Why not?"

The driver pulls up into my driveway.

"Because it's my turn to repay the favor."

I open my door and jump out before pulling her out into my arms so I can carry her into our house.

"You don't have to carry me. We aren't really married."

I scowl. "We are *really* married."

She rolls her eyes. "We aren't in love. We aren't planning on staying married. We signed a contract. We aren't *really* married."

"A prenup."

She sighs. "A contract I can already see I need to amend."

I frown, stopping before I carry her inside. "Why?"

"Because you have to stop being so nice to me all the time. I told you, I can't like you. Only the sex part. You need to be more of a jerk to me."

"I was. I walked out on you after we had sex without a word."

"And then you sent me sushi and a note, making it all better. You can't keep doing that. You need to treat me like any of the other women you fucked and didn't want a relationship with. The boundaries get too confusing otherwise. You can't do anything a boyfriend would do for me unless we are in public." Her eyes darken and her lips tense, and I know she's serious.

"No, I like treating you well."

"You need to stop. I can't handle it. That's why we keep going weeks without seeing each other. Now that we are fake married, we have to have boundaries. Mine is that we can have sex and we can do public appearances together as husband and wife. Otherwise, you treat me like a roommate that you can barely tolerate. No date nights. No sleeping in my bed. No snuggling. No watching chick flicks with me. Nothing."

I hate every single word leaving her mouth.

"And if I don't agree?"

"No more sex."

Damn, she's serious. And stubborn. I am too, but I'm not going to win this fight tonight.

"Fine."

She grins. "Now put me down. You aren't carrying me over the threshold like I'm your bride."

I grin, because she just gave me the out I was looking for. "No."

"You just agreed—"

"I agreed to treat you like a roommate and be an ass on occasion. Tonight, I'm going to be an ass. You don't want me to carry you over the threshold, but I do. Get pissed at me."

She does. The pout on her face is adorable, but it isn't gentle. She's pissed. And as much as I want to kiss her pout away, I won't. She wants me to be a jerk, which means not giving her everything she wants. She'll be begging me to be *nice* in a matter of days.

I carry her into my house. I don't bother to flip on the lights. I don't need them for what I'm about to do.

"Fine, you made your point. Now put me down."

I walk over to my sturdy dining room table with a view out into the forest.

"Fine."

I return her to her feet roughly, not waiting for her to gain her balance before I spin her around and shove her stomach onto the top of the table.

"What are you doing?" she asks.

"Fucking you."

She gasps.

I growl.

She's not going to win this war. She's not going to fall in love with me no matter what I do. I always fuck up relationships. She might as well get over this insistence that we can't be nice to each other and let me do what I want.

I undo my pants quickly, pushing them down as I hike up her dress. I've never fucked her from behind. She's never been fucked from behind. Each new thing I try with her is her first. I love being the first to teach her new things. I jerk her panties down, tearing them to rip them off her body.

She gasps again as my hand finds her pussy, flicking my thumb across her clit. She tries to move off the table, but my hand on her back keeps her down. I kick her legs apart as my cock pushes against her entrance.

"I'm going to fuck you without a condom unless you tell me to stop," I say.

She swallows at my words and takes a deep breath. "Fuck me."

I slide in, in one punishing thrust.

Larkyn cries out, grasping onto the side of the table as I slam into her.

I wait for a second, letting her get used to my cock inside her. From this angle, I can get so much deeper than before.

"This is how I fuck women who mean nothing to me," I whisper in her ear as I thrust in and out. Not touching her clit. Or building her in any way.

She bites her lip to keep from telling me to stop.

My hand reaches down between her legs and finds the bundle of nerves I know will set her off.

"This is how I fuck women I care about," I say, rubbing her clit and nibbling on her ear.

"You choose."

I stop suddenly.

She growls.

"Which will it be?"

"Make me come, you asshole."

I smile. I win this round.

I find the sweet spot again as I thrust hard until we both come.

I pull out and tuck myself back in. I just fucked a woman without a condom. A first for her and me. It felt fantastic.

She slowly climbs off the table and lowers her wedding dress to glower at me.

I cock my head to the side. "I'll show you to your bedroom. The movers finished moving you in while we were at our wedding."

I walk down the hallway to the door right next to mine. It isn't the second largest room in my house, but I wanted her close to me, even though I still plan on getting her in my bed as often as I can.

Her eyes widen when she sees the room, like I just showed her into a room fit for a queen. I guess I did compared to the place she used to occupy.

"You like it?" I ask.

She nods.

"Or you could always stay in my room tonight. I'd be happy to fuck again or snuggle if that's what you prefer."

She ignores me and runs her hands over the silk fabric of the white bedspread I bought for her. I let her keep her old bed because it is a decent bed, but the shaggy bedspread had to go.

"What happens tomorrow?" she asks.

I smile. "Tomorrow, I plan on staying home and fucking my wife as many times as she will let me."

Her eyes grow heavy with lust. She will let me fuck her plenty.

"And then, we can go shopping for a couple of dresses for events you'll be attending the rest of the month."

She frowns. "I don't need you to pay for nice dresses for me."

I sigh. Pick my battles and don't fight. "Fine. I don't have to be at work again until Tuesday. Have you found a job yet?"

She narrows her eyes. "I already have a job."

"At the yoga studio?"

She nods.

I frown. "Have you applied for any jobs, now that you graduated with a business degree? I have some openings at my company. You could come work for me. Just get me a resume, and let me know what area you are interested in working in."

"No, I have a job. I'm not going to work for you."

I study her. Something doesn't add up.

"One million dollars doesn't go as far as you think. Especially if you spend it all on dresses for events with me, instead of letting me pay for them."

She glares at me. "Don't worry; I make enough money."

"I just thought you would want to get a job in a big corporation now that you've graduated."

She falls back on her bed. "You sound like my father."

I wince. I pushed too far. "Sorry, I didn't mean to push. Just trying to understand so I know when I'll be seeing you."

She closes her eyes, and I know she'll be asleep in seconds.

I want to know what she's planning on doing with the money I gave her. Maybe then it will give me more insight into her.

"Other than sex, do you have any plans for tomorrow?"

"I'm going to run."

"But your ankle is still injured."

"I have a doctor's note saying it's safe for me to train again. I heal quickly." Her eyes and smile are bright again as she says it.

I smile and walk over to her. I pull her up so I can kiss her firmly. She melts in my arms, and I know I could convince her to sleep in my bed if I tried at all. But I'm going to respect her wishes and treat her like she's a roommate. It's the only way to convince her to sleep in my bed long-term.

I pull back, and she looks desperate for another kiss. Her body leans forward, and her eyes are still closed, waiting for another kiss that isn't coming.

"I'll see you tomorrow to train. I'll enjoy kicking your ass, roommate."

———

"I FIGURED you'd be the type to get up at five am to work-out," I say, stretching as Larkyn sits on one of my barstools with her elbows leaning on my granite counter, sipping a cup of coffee.

Larkyn narrows her eyes at me. "I am. I'm surprised you're up this early."

I grin and pour myself a cup of coffee from the pot she left on. "I also happen to be a morning person who prefers to workout in the early morning hours before most people are awake."

I lift my coffee cup to my lips. Larkyn doesn't smile at me. Her lips turn downward before she yawns.

"Tired?" I ask.

She nods.

I smile.

"Why does me being tired make you happy?"

I smirk at her deviously as I walk over to her, and lean down by her ear to whisper, even though nobody else is in the house to hear me. "Because it means I'm winning."

She scoffs and slams her coffee cup down harder than she intended to, and she winces. "Sorry. But you are not winning. I slept poorly on my first night in a new place. I always do."

"You would have slept just fine if you were in my bed."

She scowls and stands up pressing her tiny body against mine. "No, I wouldn't have, because we would have fucked all night long."

A slow smile curls up until it reaches my eyes. "You think I can last all night long?" I pause pretending to think. "You're right I can. You would have at least had a more enjoyable experience than tossing and turning all night, dreaming about me."

Finally, she takes a step back with a tiny smile of her own on her lips.

"What's that smile for?" I ask, taking another drink of my coffee while I check her body out in her running shorts and neon pink sports bra. Her abs flex with every movement of her body. Damn, I've only been awake for five minutes, and I already want to fuck her. I've never needed sex as much as when I'm around her. I pride myself on being in control of my body, and not needing sex unless I choose it.

"Nothing, just realized that I'm winning."

I frown. "It doesn't look like it from where I'm standing."

She holds her head high. "That's because you're too focused on trying to be as big of a jerk as possible until it pisses me off and I give in and want you to return to the charming man you were before. It's not going to work. I prefer a challenge. I prefer to take care of myself. I don't need you taking care of me or being nice to me. All I need is your cock at the end of the night."

I raise my eyebrows. "Only at the end of the night?"

"Yes," she breathes, but it's a lie. She wants me right now. Her breath sped up, her cheeks flushed, and her eyes glossed over with thoughts of me fucking her.

"So what does our workout consist of today? Some walking, light jogging, weight lifting, stretches, what?" I ask, trying to keep my eyes on her face instead of her abs and legs.

She smirks. "I was thinking an easy ten-mile run to warm up, and then some lifting. I saw the gym you have in the basement."

I cross my arms over my chest and glare at her. "Your doctor did not give you permission to run ten miles your first time out."

She mimics my move, crossing her arms over her chest. "She permitted me to return to my normal activities. These are my normal activities. I have a race coming up in less than a month, and I'd prefer not to get last place."

I narrow my eyes. "Fine. We will do things your way. But I'm coming with you so I can carry you home or call a cab when you're two miles in and you can't move any further. Deal?"

She rolls her eyes. "Back to worrying about me so quickly."

"I never said I wouldn't worry about you. Just that I'd be an ass rather than a gentleman. One wince from you, and I'll be carrying you over my shoulder caveman style."

She huffs. "Fine, let's go."

"You're wearing that?" I ask, when I don't see her reach for a tank top or T-shirt.

She cocks her head to the side, putting her hands on her hips and pushing her chest out. "You have a problem with what I'm wearing?"

I stare at her chest. I do. No one should see her body, but me. But now isn't the time to argue. I'll save it for when she's in pain and doesn't want me to call a car in about a mile. "Nope."

She heads out my front door, stretching her arms a little as she walks out into the dark sky. The sun has barely started to rise and provide enough light to know that it isn't the middle of the night. I predict we are back home before the sun entirely comes up. I should take her out to brunch or something. I lock the front door, turn around, and she's gone.

Dammit.

I sprint down my driveway, squinting as I look from left to right to see which direction she went. To the left is a flat stretch, to the right a giant hill. Of course, she chose the harder path. That seems to be her preferred method.

I run, chasing after her as she finishes climbing the hill. My lungs burn, and my legs ache when I finally catch her.

"What happened to warming up first?" I ask, as I inhale hard, trying to recover.

She smirks, keeping a perfect rhythm and form. She's barely out of breath despite tackling a huge hill and running expertly. She isn't jogging; she's fucking running.

"I already warmed up."

"Huh?" is all I can get out between aching pants.

"I didn't wake up at five, I woke up at four, stretched, and warmed up a little on your treadmill in the basement."

My eyes widen. "You've already been working out for an hour?"

She nods, although I don't see a drop of sweat.

"What race are you training for?" I finally ask, as she continues to sprint. I glance down at her taped ankle, but it doesn't seem to be giving her any trouble.

"The LA marathon."

I freeze, stopping for a moment to stumble and fall into my neighbor's grass.

"Come on you pansy! I don't have time to stop. I'm out of shape and need to get faster," Larkyn shouts. She doesn't hesitate for a second to stop and check on me. She just keeps running.

Shit.

I'm way out of my league. I workout. I run. I lift. I sprint. But I don't run marathons. I never have. No desire. It's too much work for not enough gain. I prefer crushing people when I take over their businesses.

I pull myself off the ground and chase after Larkyn. And I know that for the next ten miles, that is what I'm going to be doing.

Chasing her.

———

I COLLAPSE onto my sofa after the ten miles, which felt more like twenty, because Larkyn chose the hardest fucking route she could find. There were thirty-three hills on the route. Thirty-three! Insane. And she said that was her easy run day. I don't want to know what her hard day is.

I pant over and over, covered in sweat. I ditched my T-shirt somewhere around mile three. And there is no way I'm walking, or even getting in one of my cars, to go back and get it.

Larkyn walks by me, and into the kitchen. I hear her opening cabinets, and then I hear the ice as it clinks in a glass.

She walks back, and stands over me, smirking.

"I don't know how you are standing. Or moving at all," I pant.

She walks over to me and holds out a glass of water. I take it, chugging the entire glass in one gulp.

She takes a seat near my feet, and props her foot up on my ottoman before placing a bag of ice on her foot.

I raise an eyebrow. "Your ankle hurt?"

"No, but it will. I pushed it hard."

"Why?"

She stills and takes a sip of her water. I don't think she is going to answer me.

"Because I like competing against myself. I like being healthy. I like being this fit. And I like winning." She smirks at me when she says winning.

Dammit. She really does plan on winning our little battle with each other.

She smiles with her eyes as she gazes at me. "I'm surprised you were able to keep up."

I moan. "I'm not moving off this couch the rest of the week. You killed me."

"I didn't ask you to come with me. I usually prefer running on my own. No one to hold me back."

"Don't worry. I don't plan on running with you again."

She leans her head back with a massive grin on her face. She thinks she's won. One less thing for her to worry about.

"I plan on driving next to you in my car as I yell profanities at you."

Her head pops back up fast, looking at me with wide-eyes and thinned lips. She's terrified that I would really do that. And I think I just might.

Suddenly, my tastes for making her squirm change. I want to make her squirm, but for very different reasons. I'm tired of our game where I annoy the crap out of her, so she doesn't fall in love with me. I want to make her writhe under my grasp as I lick her most sensitive of parts, and taste how delicious her juices taste mixed with the sweet sweat misted over her body.

"No," she says, noticing my reaction before I say anything or move.

I laugh. "I want to taste you."

"No," she says again, her voice shaky. She wants me too, but is afraid. "I'm gross and I smell. At least let me shower first."

I smirk. "No, I want you as you are."

She takes off up the stairs. I jump off the couch, and chase after her.

She may be fast, but I'm stronger. She won't win this. I'll catch her. And when I do, I'll give her the best orgasm of her life.

Life is perfect with her. We've only been married one day, but this is precisely what I imagined. Fun. Flirting. And sex. Nothing serious.

My phone buzzes, and I glance at my Apple Watch to see the message. I freeze, not liking what it says. It's from my lawyer. All the money we deposited into her account is gone. All one million of it. I don't know what she did with the money, but I'm about to find out.

First, though, I'll fuck her. Then, I'll ask about the

money, I think, as I grab the bathroom door. She thinks she can lock herself inside and shower before I can get to her.

"You might as well give up. You're not going to win."

"Never," she squeals as I grab her.

Never. Such a meaningless word. Similar to *forever*. Neither exists. I might want her forever. I might hate her never. But both are untrue. Because as much as I thought I knew who Larkyn Day is, I'm wrong. She tricked me into giving her money she desperately needed for something. And if I'm not careful, she's going to take more from me. More money, more of my time, more of my heart. Until there is nothing left, but an empty shell.

I thought I married her to keep women like her away, but what if she is the devil I've been trying to save myself from all along?

KADE IS GOING TO WIN.

Not the war, but this fight.

He catches my arm, and I freeze. I don't want him to fuck me when I'm this gross. I don't want him to find me disgusting and think I usually smell like this. If he fucks me now, it will be a long time before he fucks me again.

I sweat a lot when I run. And that sweat smells like ass. As much as it would help me if he suddenly didn't want to have sex with me anymore, I don't think that I could survive a whole year in his house with him without sex.

My heart is conflicted though as he pulls me close. I want to fuck him, but I also don't know whether to knee him in the balls or thank him for running with me. I hate him acting like he can control me, which is what he was doing running with me. He thought he could persuade me to stop.

But I also want to thank him for giving me the motivation to keep running. That hurt like a motherfucker, but it was necessary if I'm going to get back into marathon shape.

"Tell me no," Kade says, as I'm pressed against his body,

straddling the doorway between the bathroom and my bedroom.

"No."

He smirks, knowing that I would say no.

I take a breath, trying to calm my breathing so I can keep a clear head.

He takes a step back, not touching me, but still close enough I can smell the sweat dripping off his body. He grins to show me his damn dimples, and my legs go weak.

I grab the doorframe to stay upright, when I want to be holding onto him.

"Tell me to leave," he says.

"Lea—"

He grabs my shorts and shoves them down. Kneels before me and grabs my thighs while his mouth attacks my pussy.

Jesus.

He lifts me up as my legs go around his shoulders, and his tongue dances across my bud. I grab his head tightly to remind myself to hold on and not let my head fall backward like I want, as noises leave my mouth I didn't know existed.

He drops me on my bed and kneels at the edge as his head comes down on my pussy again. He nips at my clit.

I bite my lip to keep him from knowing how much I like what he's doing.

"Tell me to stop," he breathes against the lips between my legs.

"Don't you dare stop!" I arch my back until my body is pressed against his mouth again.

He smirks and attacks. His tongue moves faster, matching the pulse of my blood, which is all pooled between my legs instead of in my head.

I come, screaming Kade's damn name.

He wipes his mouth with the back of his hand as he climbs up my body.

"Don't you ever tell me, or any man, not to fuck you because you think you are gross. You are fucking amazing. Even more amazing after you just kicked my ass running ten miles. Don't you dare. Promise?" His lips twitch as he talks and the smile I'm so used to vanishes. He's serious, and I'm afraid he won't let me off the bed until I've taken his oath.

"I promise."

He stills, and when he finally believes my words, he leans back. He climbs back on my bed making himself comfortable, smiling with his arms behind his head, so that I can see every glorious inch of his toned body all the way to the v-shape that disappears beneath his shorts, hiding the one part of his body mine is still aching for.

"Good, now fuck me to prove you don't find me gross."

Damn, that slow smile is contagious.

I pull the bra off my body and attack. My legs part over his legs and I lower myself until I find the hardness push against my groin like I was expecting. Our lips lock, and I taste his sweat mixed with my cum.

It's the opposite of gross. It's what pleasure, pain, hard work, and desire taste like. How could that taste bad? More importantly, how could I have ever thought that he would find me gross? He can't resist me, just like I can't resist his glistening body.

I can't wait to have him in me. He knows I can't either.

His pants are down, and I feel his slick cock against my entrance.

He doesn't wait for me to permit him to fuck me without a condom this time. He just does. And I don't blame him. Fucking without a barrier is so much hotter than fucking with one.

I thrust on top of him. Loving being in control of everything. Speed. Depth. Angles. And controlling when Kade gets to come. Because I plan on torturing him a little, just like he has me.

I stop suddenly, pretending I need to catch my breath.

"Not happening, sweetie. You don't get to taunt me. You forget I'm more experienced at this than you." Kade starts thrusting.

I pout. I forgot that he can thrust from underneath me just as easily as he can on top.

He kisses me again, and the pout melts away.

He nibbles on my lips as he comes inside me, just as my body pulses my orgasm around him.

He collapses back, exhausted. But that just energized me more. *Who knew sex would turn me into a sex fiend?*

"We have to wait at least another twenty minutes before we do that again. You exhaust me, woman."

I smile.

"I need to go lift anyway." I consider staying and asking him about why we aren't using a condom. But it doesn't matter. I'm on birth control, and I'm clean. And as much as I don't want to admit it, I trust Kade. I trust him too much.

I start to climb off of him, but Kade grabs my hand stopping me.

"I have a question first."

I pause and sit back down on his cock that is just beginning to stir again. *Twenty minutes, my ass.*

"What did you do with the money?"

"How do you know?"

"I have my ways."

"You have lawyers and people that work at the bank you mean?"

He shrugs.

I frown. *Why is he asking me about the money? And why does he seem so pissed about it?* I open my mouth to tell him what I did with the money, but then I stop.

"It's none of your business what I did with the money." I climb off of him. He tries to keep me on him, but I jerk my arm free and stand next to my bed pissed. Butt naked, but pissed.

"Yes, it is my business. It's my money. You are my wife. I need to know if you did anything illegal or if you are going to need more. Because if you already spent everything, I don't know how you expect to buy things like dresses to the parties you are supposed to be attending with me."

I glare at him. I've never been so angry with him before. If he's doing this to keep up his end of the deal of being an ass, then he's doing a good job. Seconds ago, I could have loved him for making me feel wanted. Now there is nothing but hate.

"I didn't do anything illegal. And don't worry about the dresses. I'll make sure I wear something worthy of being your wife, and you won't have to pay me another dime."

"Tell me what you did with the money."

"No. It's none of your business. Our contract never had any stipulations about me telling you what I did with the money or that I had to spend it a certain way." I grab a new pair of shorts and bra and put them on. "Now, I'm going to lift. Enjoy the rest of your day, you bastard."

———

"DAMN, I need to spend more time in the gym. Or at least I

need to watch my back, because I'm pretty sure my wife could beat me up," Kade says, standing in the doorway of the basement gym as I push the bar with way too much weight on it over my head.

I should have taken today easy. I haven't lifted in weeks, and my wrist is still fragile. But Kade pissed me off. So I taped up my wrist and went full out. I'll regret it later.

"What do you want?" I ask, racking the bar and sitting up to wipe the sweat from my forehead, not even bothering to look at Kade. I'm too tired to give him my full glare.

I hear him walk toward me, but I keep my eyes focused on the floor like the black spongy material that makes up the floor is interesting.

"You don't even have any music playing or the TV on," Kade says, stopping next to me.

I turn to him and snarl. "I couldn't figure out how to work your ridiculous sound system, and I don't watch much TV. I don't need entertainment to workout."

He grins, displaying his damn dimples. He's changed. He's wearing dark jeans and a black T-shirt that fits him too well. My insides curl, and my heart speeds up. *How the hell does he melt my anger for him with just a grin? I really am in trouble.*

I lower my eyebrows and frown. He doesn't get to know what he's doing to me.

I lean back down and lift the bar off the rack. I've already finished my reps, but I need a distraction from the sex god that is standing over me looking at me like he can control all my emotions.

My arms wobble a little as I lower the bar to my chest.

"I need your help," Kade says, putting his hands in his pocket.

My eyes cut to him as I push the bar up. He looks so

sincere. Innocent, even. His eyes are big, and he bites his lip, like he can't believe he even admitted that to me.

I lower the bar again to my chest, and this time, I can barely push the bar up. Kade grabs it as my arms wobble, and he helps me rack the bar.

I pant heavily, but I'm not sure if it's because I'm tired or want Kade to climb on top of me and fuck me on this bench.

"I need you to bartend with me tonight at King's," Kade says.

I smirk. "No."

He sighs rubbing his neck. "I figured you would say that."

"Then you are learning. Why would I want to help you out?"

"Because you are my wife, and I'm paying you to help me."

I snarl. I hate Kade. I don't know how I go from liking to hating so quickly.

"Well, that has me convinced." I roll my eyes.

"Please?"

"No."

"Why not? What else are you going to do tonight?"

I get up and walk over to the large tank of water and fill a paper cup with water before washing it down. I feel his eyes on my ass, and when I turn around, they are on my flattened breasts, squashed beneath the sports bra I'm wearing.

I raise my eyebrows. "Really? You're checking me out while asking me for help? That's not going to work."

He cocks his head and smiles, as he purposefully stares harder at my breasts.

"Just honoring our contract and making sure you hate me. Is it working?"

I toss the empty cup into the trashcan. "Yes."

"Good, now go shower. You have ten minutes, and we need to leave."

"I'm not helping you."

"Yes, you are. I've been far too nice to you lately. I need the opportunity to make you mad at me." He wiggles his eyebrows.

I giggle. *Dammit, no.*

He chuckles. "See, you like me way too much right now. A night of me bossing you around ought to fix that."

I sigh. Kade's right. I need to be angry. And I don't exactly have anything to do tonight unless you count taking a long bath and icing my entire body all night to make the soreness go away.

"Fine."

His eyes twinkle at my surrender.

"Good, now shower and put on jeans and a black shirt. You have five minutes until we leave."

I frown. "I thought I had ten."

He shrugs. "Four now."

"I hate you," I say, racing past him to go shower.

"I know."

12 KADE

FUCKING SEBASTIAN.

I'm going to kill him.

That's all I could think about when I got the phone call from Axel, my best friend, and manager of most of my bars, telling me Sebastian didn't show up tonight. Sebastian is supposed to be managing this bar. I'm giving him an opportunity to learn before he takes it over from Axel and me. But if he keeps being a no-show, he'll be lucky if I let him run a lemonade stand.

I throw my arm around Larkyn's shoulder as I lead her into one of my favorite places in the world. I stare at her face, as hard as it is for me to pull my eyes away from her ass in her skin tight jeans, or her breasts in her black T-shirt. Or the curl that has fallen out of her perfect bun.

Instead, I gaze at her gorgeous makeup-free face. She yelled at me and said she didn't even have time to put makeup on before I demanded that we leave. But she's the type of woman I doubt would wear makeup anyway. And I'm glad she's isn't wearing any. It shows off her freckles and sun-kissed cheeks.

"Welcome to King's," I say, opening the door for her. I try to keep my voice level, so she doesn't realize the importance of the place, and I can get her honest reaction.

We stop just inside, and Larkyn soaks everything in. Her gaze floats around the bubbles of tables scattered throughout the room. The triple high ceiling that makes the bar look more significant than it is. And the booths that sit on the edge of the floors above, giving the perfect view of the dance floor below.

A slow smile spreads on her face, and a twinkle sparks in her eyes.

My heart beats again, seeing her expression. She likes the place.

She bites her lip as she finally tears her eyes away from the sparkle of the room to me. "This is your favorite place in the world, isn't it?"

I narrow my eyes. "No," I lie.

She smirks and stares back at the room that is alive with people, despite it only being seven in the evening. This place usually doesn't start getting crowded until nine.

"It's fantastic. I usually prefer to be alone, but this place makes me feel alive, more than I've felt in years."

I grin. "It's my second favorite place in the world."

She laughs. "I knew it. What's your first?"

I shake my head and place my hand on the small of her back. "I'd tell you, but it'd make you fall in love with me."

She licks her bottom lip slowly. "Oh, yea? I doubt that."

"Good of you to finally show up," Axel says, holding a tray of empty glasses.

I shrug. "I had to wait for Larkyn to shower. I figured we could use the extra help."

Axel rakes his eyes over Larkyn. I know he's doing it to piss me off, but I'll still kick his ass later. I hold Larkyn closer to me and look down at her finger to notice she's wearing her engagement ring with her wedding ring. Good, I need her to be mine tonight.

"Make sure you keep this one in line tonight. Kade hasn't bartended in ages." Axel winks at Larkyn.

Larkyn laughs. "I'll make sure Kade works his butt off."

"Good. Nice to see you again Larkyn." Axel leans over and kisses her on the cheek.

I glare at him like I'm about to punch him in the face. He smirks as he finishes the kiss.

"I've got to go. It seems one of the waitresses and both of our best bartenders called in sick all in the same night. We need you to cover the main bar," Axel says, before walking away.

Larkyn's eyes follow him, and she blushes a little. Axel's good looking. He's tall, with a beard and a man bun to go with his muscular physique. But she's mine, not his.

"Are you done ogling my best friend, wifey?"

She cocks her head to look at me. "Are you jealous?"

"No, just reminding you that you are *my wife*. So start acting like it."

She shakes her head. "You got this being a jerk thing down."

I sigh. "Come on, let's get you set up at the bar."

I show her the bar, where everything is, and how to work the cash register.

And then we both get swept away with a barrage of people.

"Larkyn, I need you to make two old fashioneds, a lemon drop, a manhattan, and two cosmos. That is if you know how to make all of those," I say.

She gives me her best 'I'm going to punch you later'

stare while beginning to get the glasses out for the most complicated drinks anyone could order.

I'm busy pouring five beers for the men sitting at the bar.

"Seriously?" she asks, eyeing me as the sticky syrupy sugar from the lemon drop gets all over her hands.

I finish pouring the beers and hand them to the two guys.

"What?" I ask, faking innocent.

She slides the two old fashioneds to me and carries the lemon drop and manhattan to the other two men waiting.

She smiles at them a little too brightly, and when one of the men hands her his credit card, she lets her hand stroke his hand for just a second first.

I growl as I follow her to the cash register.

"Not cool," I growl in her ear. "You're mine. Remember?"

She bites her lip trying to hold back a grin. "Then start making some of the complicated drinks yourself. You can start by making two cosmos for those women standing over there. I need to wash my hands. I'm tired of getting sticky sugar all over my hands from all the sweet drinks these women keep ordering."

I press my lips against her ear. "I'll make the drinks if you stop flirting with the customers."

Her breath catches. "If I stop flirting, I don't make as many tips."

My tongue traces around the edge of her ear. "If you keep flirting, I'm going to throw you over my shoulder, carry you to the bathroom, and fuck you until you remember, you're *mine*."

Her teeth rake over her bottom lip. "Then, I'll definitely keep flirting."

I growl. I should have said something less sexy, although I'm desperate to fuck Larkyn in the bathroom. The first break we get, that's precisely what I'm doing. *Where is Axel when I need him?*

I release Larkyn as I head over to make the two cosmos. When I finish, I carry them down the bar to the two waiting women.

"Sorry for the wait," I say, sliding the drinks across the bar to the two blonde beauties.

"I'd wait forever to be served by you," one of the women says, as she strokes my forearm and bats her eyelashes at me.

"I'm Jane." She takes a sip of her drink. "This is delicious, how did you make it?" She leans forward, flashing me her cleavage.

I cock my head to the side with a smile, knowing that Larkyn is watching me. I'm about to piss her off.

"I'd love to show you exactly how I make it," I say, winking at her as I lean in.

I feel hands on my chest from behind me. I stare down at the ring that Larkyn has strategically placed firmly on my chest so there is no way Jane could miss it.

"Hello, hubby," Larkyn says, turning my face toward her before she kisses me on the lips, making sure she slides her tongue into my mouth.

She breaks away as she grins seductively at me, before turning her attention to the two women. "Can we get you two anything?" Larkyn asks, staring the women down.

"Nope," Jane says awkwardly, as she and her friend carry their drinks away.

Larkyn frowns at me.

"What? I make better tips if I flirt a little," I say, repeating her words.

"Fine, no more flirting from either of us."

I grab her at the waist as she tries to leave to take another man's order. I pull her to me and kiss her again. I can't get enough of her lips. Her sweet, perfume. Her moans. I can never get enough of her.

She pulls away with a dreamy look on her face. She can't get enough of me either.

I swat her ass as she walks away to make more drinks.

The night continues, and we both continue teasing each other. Bossing each other around while flirting and kissing any chance we get.

A crowd forms and I have to move fast to keep up. I haven't talked to Larkyn in half an hour. Nor flirted or kissed or even brushed against her. We've been too busy. Finally, I get a break when a group of guys orders shots of tequila. I glance across the bar to check on Larkyn.

Larkyn brings a man his whiskey with a scowl on her face.

I frown, but try to be patient. I know Larkyn can handle herself with touchy men. I've seen her do it all night. And as much as I want to jump in and defend her honor, I don't. I've pushed her far enough tonight, and I don't want to push too far and not get to fuck her tonight.

But then he grips her arm far too tightly and pulls her chest over the bar and kisses her.

Hell no.

I storm across the bar toward the man whose lips press against my wife's. She tries to push him away, but he digs his fingers deeper into her arm.

I push him away from her, and then before I can think, my fist makes contact with his face. Blood pours from his nose, but it's not enough. I punch him again.

The man laughs as he steps out of reach before I punch him again.

"I'm going to sue. I should get a pretty penny for getting punched by royalty like you."

"Get the fuck out!" I yell.

The man laughs. I look over at Axel who motions for our security team to grab him and take him out. Two of my security guys catch the man and start walking him out. The man grins as blood drips down his face and he flashes a look to Larkyn behind me.

Good thing I have a security team to handle creeps like this or I might have ended up in jail tonight after I killed him. I need to get a grip on myself if I would kill someone just for kissing Larkyn.

"Man, that guy was creepy," I say, joking as I turn to face Larkyn who I assume is going to give me a hard time for punching the guy instead of letting her handle him herself.

That's not what I see.

Larkyn's frozen. Her eyes are wide and unblinking. Her mouth tightens into a grimace. And her face is pale white.

"Larkyn, are you okay?" I ask, moving in front of her as I put my arms on her biceps. I try gently shaking like that would someone get rid of the shock she's in.

It doesn't work.

"Larkyn?" I ask, my voice catching in my throat.

Something is seriously wrong.

"Larkyn, talk to me. What's going on?"

Silence.

She does finally blink. Otherwise, she's still frozen. She's not going to talk to me here.

The bar has started to slow down, as it's well past midnight, but there are still plenty of people hanging around the bar looking for drinks.

I motion to Axel who delivers two drinks to one of his tables and then jogs over to us.

"Take over for us," I say.

Axel takes one look at Larkyn, and he does as I say, hopping into the bar.

I wrap my arms around Larkyn's shoulders and lead her to the manager's office in the back. I get her to sit on the couch, and then I close the door behind me, making sure to lock it before I take a seat next to her.

And then I wait. I stroke her hair and hold her hand and hope that whatever just happened back there didn't break her. Because I'm not ready to give her up yet. If she's broken, she won't want to stay mine.

"I hate him," are the words that finally leave her mouth.

I exhale and sink back into the couch, still searching her eyes for signs of life. Her cheeks have pinked, her lips are moist, and her breathing is steady.

"I hate him, too," I say, with a tiny smile.

"I shouldn't have let him get to me like that."

"No." I grab her face so that she can see how entirely wrong she is. This is not her fault. "Don't blame yourself for anything. He kissed you. He touched you. However you reacted, is perfectly acceptable. He was in the wrong, not you."

She nods, but her eyes say she doesn't agree with me.

I frown. I don't know how to get through to her. "You're plenty strong. You don't have to punch every guy that hurts you, though. That's why you have me."

A tear falls down her cheek. I rub it when it hits my thumb.

"Hey, it's okay. You're okay," I say, pulling her into my lap so that I can hold her as firmly as I want.

She starts bawling, and I don't understand. Larkyn is

fierce, strong, invincible. She didn't cry when her father said she was worthless. She didn't cry when she was in agonizing pain in the hospital. She didn't cry when she injured her leg. But she's crying now. Full sobs. That man was way out of line, but it was just a kiss. I don't understand why she would be this upset.

And then it hits me. Larkyn was raped. Of course, a man touching her without her permission would upset her.

I hold her tighter, hating that I put her in this position, and didn't immediately try to protect her.

"His name is Nathan Watts."

I slowly ease back so that I can look at her as she speaks. "You know him?"

She nods and swallows like it's hard to get the next words out. "He was...he raped me."

My eyes widen, and my body chills as she speaks. I should talk. Say something. But now I've lost the ability to speak.

"We used to date. Freshman year. It was serious. I was madly in love with him."

Now my heart has stopped. Because it feels like someone has stabbed me when she mentions loving another guy, yet doesn't ever want to love me.

"But I was young. I wanted to take things slowly. Nathan was a senior. I was a freshman. I didn't want to jump into bed with him. We dated two months before I was ready."

I narrow my eyes, not understanding how it ended so badly if she was in love with this guy. How she was even still a virgin when I had her.

"Nathan was taking me to a party. I think it might have even been one of your parties. Anyway, I got all dressed up and decided that night was the night. We went to dinner, stopped by the party for about five minutes, and then he took me back to his apartment."

I nod, needing to hear the end of this story more than I need to breathe.

"And then, I changed my mind. It just didn't feel right. I wanted to wait a little longer. I said I'd had too much to drink, which was true, and I felt sick. I didn't want my first time to be when I was drunk.

"Nathan disagreed. He wouldn't stop. I fought for about five seconds before I grew still. I couldn't move. Or breathe. I didn't even tell him to stop."

She looks me in the eye. "Just like tonight."

"No." I stroke her again, feeling her wet, tear-stained cheeks. "You did not have to say no. He knew that you didn't want him to kiss you. Just like he knew you didn't want to have sex with him. This is not your fault."

She nods and smiles as a tear falls down her cheek again. And I can't help myself. She's so beautiful. She thinks she's weak right now, but I've never seen her stronger.

I lean down and kiss her tenderly on the lips, as the tears that have fallen over her cheeks cover her mouth. The tears continue, and I know I need to stop. This isn't what she needs right now. She needs comfort, not a man to grope her.

I pull back. "I'm sorry."

She sucks in a breath, and I think she's going to start bawling again, or yell at me for kissing her when she needed me to be her friend.

Her body tenses.

Fuck, I screwed up.

Her arms grab my cheeks, and her lips attack mine. Her tongue pushes into my mouth. Her body lands on mine.

"Don't ever tell me you are sorry for kissing me again. You are the only thing keeping me grounded. I don't usually like men that punch other men, but what you did for me... what you're doing for me now. I've never been more turned on in my life."

She bites her lip and then she grabs my shirt and lifts it off. I see the twinkle return to her eyes when she stares down at my chest. I did something right for once.

"I'm so glad you were my first," she says pulling her shirt off, revealing a far too sexy bra.

I growl. "I'm happy you're my first wife."

She laughs.

I smirk, as comfortable as it would be to fuck her on the couch, it just isn't enough.

"What?" she asks, smiling at my mischievous look.

"I'm going to fuck you on the desk."

She eyes the desk behind me covered in papers and electronics.

"No, we can't. We might break it or—"

I plant my lips on hers as I lift her up. Her legs wrap around my waist while I carry her over to the desk without protest.

And then, I sweep everything off into a mound on the floor.

"Oh my god!" Larkyn squeals.

I grin, loving the sound falling from her lips.

"You did not just do that," Larkyn says, laughing.

"I did. This is my bar. I can do what I want."

She stares down at the computer, which hardly has a scratch on it.

"What if we broke it?"

I kiss her again as I lower her to the desk. "Then, I'll buy a new one."

"Simple as that, huh? Just throw some money at it and problem fixed."

I look into her eyes, knowing that she thinks that's how I fix all of my problems including any I have with her.

"When the problem is simple, yes. Anything more complicated requires a kiss from you."

She hooks her legs around me and pulls my body to her as she kisses me. I'm usually not the kind of guy that cares much about the kiss, except that it leads to the much more enjoyable part. The sex part.

But when Larkyn kisses me, I lose my damn mind. I don't think about anything else. I feel the kiss everywhere in my body. And I moan like it's the only reaction my body can ever muster.

I grab her jeans and undo them expertly with one hand, while never having to glance down at what I'm doing and stop kissing Larkyn.

I kiss down her chest as my hand slips underneath the delicate thong she's wearing.

She is hot in anything, but seeing her in these lacey things makes her even hotter. Knowing that she is wearing them for me almost makes me come without fucking her.

When I kiss back up her body, she stops me just before I get to her lips by pressing her finger to my lips.

"How did I get so lucky to find someone like you?"

I shake my head and then nibble on her finger. "I'm the lucky one."

She moans, and I undo my pants releasing my cock before settling between her legs.

"Fuck me, Kade," she says, knowing tonight I need her explicit permission.

At her words, I slide inside, filling her as her moans fill the room.

I kiss her hard while I fuck her, taking with me all the pain and heartache she's feeling. I don't want her ever to feel that way again. I need to protect her. I won't let another man hurt her ever. Including me.

So as much as a new feeling is floating up through my body making me feel things toward Larkyn that I didn't think were possible, I push them back down. I will not feel anything more than I already do toward Larkyn. I can't.

"Come, beautiful. Let go of the pain."

She does, and it's the most exquisite sound that leaves her mouth. I genuinely think she let go in that moment. I come right after her, filling her with my cum.

When we finish, I carry her back to the couch and pick up her clothes, handing them to her. We both get dressed as I stare at her beautiful flushed body and the smile that hasn't left her lips since she came.

"How are you feeling?" I ask.

She bites her lip and yanks at my shirt, pulling me toward her. "Like you're the best husband ever."

I grin, but when I look into her eyes and see something more, I know I've fucked up. I quickly stand before her.

"I need to call my friends at the police department and see if I can get Nathan locked up, or at least a restraining order so that he can't come around you anymore."

She sighs. "Thank you. You can try. Nathan got out of prison a couple of weeks ago, so maybe that will help."

I kiss her, needing to take away the memory.

"He went to prison after he raped you?" I ask.

She shakes her head and stares at me with her big eyes as she curls up on the couch like she might fall asleep.

"No. I reported him, but they didn't have enough evidence to arrest him. Especially since we were dating. It was just his word against mine. But the police did a thorough investigation, and it turned out, he was selling pot and cocaine. He went to prison for possession."

I frown. I hate that she never got her justice. I know there isn't much I can do now, but I have enough connections to get a restraining order.

I pull out my phone. "I'm going to make a couple of calls and see what I can do to fix this. Then, I'll take you home."

I lean down and kiss her on the forehead.

She smiles up at me. "Thank you, hubby."

I swallow as she calls me hubby again. She likes calling me her husband or hubby. I love hearing it fall from her lips, but it's a problem. I promised I wouldn't hurt her. And right now the way we both feel, I'm going to hurt her.

I step outside the office to make the calls to protect her. Tonight, I can be her prince. But tomorrow, I need to bring back the ass she hates. After hearing her story tonight, it's more important than ever that I keep her from falling in love with me. She deserves better than a man who only cares about money, his work, and getting laid.

13 LARKYN

THE LAST FEW weeks have crept by. Kade has mostly left me alone. He's been busy working, while I've tried to teach as many yoga classes as possible to save as much money as I can. After teaching, I've spent most of my time training for the race today. Or hanging out with Serena. I need to stop meeting up with Serena though. All she wants to talk about is Kade.

Are we serious? Do I like him? Have I fallen in love?

It's exhausting. I can't handle talking to her anymore.

But I miss Kade. He's been traveling for work weekly. And even when is home, he's been working late. He's barely even made time to fuck me. I don't know how he has so much restraint. I've spent every night in this big empty house touching myself, making myself come. But it is nothing like when Kade fucks me.

And somehow, Nathan is back in prison. I don't know what he did, but Kade called me a couple of days after his release and said Nathan violated his parole and is back in prison.

I toss my running shoes into my bag and zip it shut. I swing the bag over my shoulder as I hear a knock on my bedroom door.

I grin. *Kade.*

"Come in."

Kade opens the door slowly and moves just inside my doorway. He's dressed in jeans and a buttoned-down shirt.

My smile drops from my face, and I almost drop the bag from my shoulder; the sight of his outfit knocks me so off balance. He's not coming to see me race.

"I wanted to pop in to wish you luck today. Sorry, I can't make it to your race today. Work calls."

I nod and give him a fake smile. But I can't say thank you. I don't open my mouth at all, because if I do, I know what's going to come out. True feelings that I don't want Kade to know about.

He hesitates in my doorway, before walking over to me, squeezing my body against his, and wrapping his arms around my back. My face buries in his chest. I smell the familiar musk of his aftershave. And I almost tell him to hell with the race and work. I need him to fuck me right now. Against the wall. In the bed. On the floor for all I care. I need his cock.

But he releases me before I have a chance to kiss him. If I had brushed my lips against his, everything would be different.

I didn't.

So now, Kade is walking away, out of my bedroom.

"Good luck, Larkyn. Text me how the race goes." And then he's out my bedroom door as he presses his phone to his ear to take a call. He doesn't even want me to call him afterward, just text. That's how much I mean to him.

I thought after Kade punched Nathan, I meant more to

him than just a fake relationship where I help him fend off women. Apparently, not. I'm not even sure he thinks he needs me around to fend off women anymore, since we haven't been out in public in weeks.

I head to my old Toyota Corolla and drive off to the race. It's five in the morning. I didn't even ask Kade what he's doing up this early. But I guess running a billion dollar empire requires Kade to work all hours of the day and night.

———

AS I'M RUNNING the race, all I can think about is Kade.

Kade, treating me like a queen.

Kade, being an ass.

Kade, in his sexy suits.

Kade, naked in my bed.

Kade, bossing me around.

Kade, comforting me when I cry.

He's a distraction. From everything. I should be focused on my pace, form, and where I'm planting my feet.

But I can't stop.

All I think about is Kade's grin.

His dimples.

His giant eyes, staring at me lovingly. Like I'm really his. But I'm not.

Shit...

My body crashes into the concrete, as my ankle twists beneath my body.

Fuck.

Runners jump around me, not bothering to stop and check on me. I don't blame them. They want to win. Get sponsors, same as me.

I glance down at my fitness watch, tracking my pace

and mileage. Nine miles in a record pace. I could have won. Or at least finished in the top five.

Now, my dreams are gone.

I will never win a marathon. My body will heal eventually, but my heart isn't in it anymore. I like running. It used to be my whole life, but now all I can think about is Kade. I've turned into my mother. The one person I hate for not having her own life.

I need more.

But how can I, when my entire life revolves around Kade?

I don't know. But I need to get my shit together.

I force myself up into a standing position. Gravel and rocks fall from my body as I dust myself off. I hop on my good leg as a tear trickles down my cheek toward the nearest first aid station.

I'm not sad that my running career is over. Running made me feel alive, but it didn't serve the purpose of helping other people.

I'm sad that I don't know what comes next or how to go about achieving my purpose of helping other people. I love teaching yoga, but I hardly earn enough to feed myself. I don't need much money, but I need more than the thousand dollars I earn a month.

"Let me help you," a man in a red first aid shirt says, draping my arm over his shoulders.

"Thanks," I say, faking a smile at the good-looking man. Usually, I would be entranced with a man like him. Especially with my arm draped over his shoulders and our bodies so close together. Today, I feel nothing. I feel like a sex addict, but the only man that can quench my thirst is Kade.

"I'm Jeremy," the man says.

"Larkyn."

He smiles. "Sit here, Larkyn." He pulls up a folding chair behind me.

I ease myself down onto the chair as Jeremy lifts my leg up so he can inspect my ankle. He slowly removes my shoes, as my swollen ankle reddens.

"You need to have it looked at by a doctor."

I nod.

"Anyone I should call to help you get home?"

I shake my head. "Call me a cab. I'll pick up my car later."

Jeremy frowns, but pulls out his phone.

"I can take you home," Sebastian's voice rings out behind me.

Jeremy looks from Sebastian back to me. He raises an eyebrow, asking me without words if he should leave me alone with the man.

I smile at Jeremy, who walks over to a table a few feet away and starts organizing supplies.

"What are you doing here?" I ask, as Sebastian squats in front of me. He doesn't look good. His hair is disheveled, and he needs a haircut. His eyes are bloodshot. His clothes have dirt stains. And his breath reeks of alcohol.

"I came to apologize."

I exhale. I don't know why he doesn't make me anxious. Maybe because he's so good looking or that I almost slept with him. I don't know.

"That's nice of you Sebastian, but I'm not looking for an apology. I think you need to focus on getting the help you need and taking care of yourself."

"Please, Larkyn, I need to..." Sebastian stumbles over my leg as he stands up.

I wince as he hits my ankle and his hands flail, trying to grab onto my shoulders to keep his balance.

Before I realize what is happening, Sebastian is knocked on his ass, lying on the ground.

Blood spews from his lip, as a fist comes down on his face again. Sebastian holds his hands up to protect his face, but he doesn't fight back.

"Don't ever touch Larkyn again. You understand?" Kade says.

Kade.

My eyes widen as I grasp my injured ankle. I don't know whether I'm happy or afraid to see Kade here. I'm happy that's he's here. He lied to me and came to my race. But the way he's looking at his brother terrifies me.

Kade's eyes are dark, his face red, and fist balled, while his other hand tightens around Sebastian's throat.

"We are through Sebastian. You're on your own. I'm tired of fixing things for you. Don't call me asking for my help anymore. Don't ask me for money. Don't ask me to even be there for you as your brother. I'm done helping you," Kade says.

Kade huffs out a breath through his nose, and it might as well be fire. He finally turns toward me after taking more breaths to calm himself down. While Sebastian, is still in a heap on the ground. Several of the medics are staring at the scene, not sure if they should help Sebastian or stay out of it.

"You okay?" Kade asks me.

I nod.

"Sebastian didn't hurt me, and my ankle was already hurt."

"Your ankle, okay?"

"I twisted it. It will be fine. I just need to rest it."

Kade stares down at my ankle with the same intensity one might stare at a bomb waiting for it to go off.

"I'm fine," I say again.

Kade grimaces at me and then scoops me up in his arms.

I don't fight with him. Even if I could walk, I wouldn't argue with him. I like him carrying me. I like being in his arms again. Just being near him.

"You lied to me," I say.

He ignores me. "Where did you park?"

"The west parking lot."

He swallows, and I can hear him breathe, each breath strong and deep as we walk.

"Why did you come and not tell me?"

"Because I didn't want you to think I like you."

"You like me?" I ask with a smile.

"Of course, but that's all it is. *Like*."

My eyes drop. I don't want him to see the pain in my eyes.

"You were too harsh on Sebastian. He didn't even touch me. You don't need to punch every guy that touches me."

He growls, and I know he disagrees.

Kade helps me into my car, and then he goes to the driver's seat.

"Home?" he asks.

"Drop me off at the yoga studio. I said I would help with any classes after I finished my race."

His eyes widen, and he rubs his head. But it looks more like he's doing something with his hands to keep from strangling me.

"No."

He doesn't say anything else. Just a no.

"No? You don't get to tell me what to do."

"When you are acting crazy and may have just had a concussion, then I do."

I frown, but don't argue. Honestly, I want to spend the rest of the day with Kade.

"You're lucky I'm not taking you straight to the doctor."

"It's just a sprain. I'm fine."

He rolls his eyes as more steam leaves his nostrils.

My car makes a weird noise as Kade speeds up, ending the silence that has spread between us.

"You need to buy a new car. This one is about to break down any minute."

I frown. "I happen to like my car."

"Buy a new one."

"No."

He sighs and rubs his neck again.

"Why did you punch Sebastian? I want the truth."

He keeps driving, ignoring me, and I give up pushing. It seems that we aren't on the same page anymore. We can't even carry on a simple conversation.

Kade pulls the car into the driveway of his house, and he shuts off the engine, but doesn't get out to help me. I sit too and wait. I could hop in the house on my good leg, but I don't want to. I want Kade's arms around me again.

"Our father died when I was fifteen. Sebastian was only twelve. Lung cancer."

I suck in a breath as Kade finally speaks.

"I'm so sorry," I say.

He stares into my eyes and touches my cheek like he needs my touch to be strong enough to continue speaking.

"Our father was abusive. He wasn't a nice man. Sebastian and I were happy to see him gone."

I place my hand on his, trying to bring him comfort.

"My mother though..." He takes a deep breath. "From

what I remember about her, she was amazing. She divorced my father when I was six. She didn't have anything. No money. No job. No skills. But she loved Sebastian and I. Fought for custody of us. But she didn't have the means to fight our father's numerous lawyers."

I tighten my grip on his hand.

"She died of a broken heart."

A tear trickles down my cheek. He hurts. So much. And I can't do anything to make it better.

"Sebastian started acting out after our father died. He partied. Drank, smoked weed. All of it.

"I thought it was just a phase that would pass. But he's never been able to get over our parents' deaths or the emotional abuse he suffered from our father.

"I don't know how to help Sebastian. I don't think I can help him. I know I should give up on him, but I can't keep fighting for him when he keeps screwing up."

His voice trembles and breaks, as tears slip down his cheek.

I grab his head and cradle him against my chest, crying as well. I open my mouth numerous times, trying to find words to comfort him, but there are no words. Nothing I can say will make any of it better. I want to say Sebastian will get better. With help, he'll clean up his life. But I don't know that.

So instead, I get out of the car, walking tenderly on my injured foot to Kade's side, and I lead Kade out of my car and into the house. His eyes are sad, but he doesn't fight me. Tonight, it's my turn to take care of him.

I guide him slowly to his bedroom until he's sitting on the edge of the bed. Then, I remove his shoes. Followed by his jeans and shirt.

I remove my running shorts and bra, and pull on one of

his T-shirts before climbing into the bed next to him and snuggling against his chest.

This is the first time I've slept in his bed, since the first time he fucked me. Tonight isn't about sex. Tonight is about comforting a man I'm falling for.

14 KADE

LARKYN IS an angel when she sleeps. Her head is curled up against my chest as her arm and leg are draped over my waist.

I've never slept with a woman in my bed before without having sex with her first. It was exactly what I needed. A night holding a woman I care about.

But it makes my feelings for her confused. *What am I supposed to do now?*

Tell her I'm falling in love with her, and I want to try a relationship for real? Or keep trying to push her away every time we do something that moves toward getting too close?

I run my hand through her sweaty hair. My lips curl up. She really does reek. She never showered after her race yesterday. She just curled up in my bed with me and made my pain go away.

If I were a better man, I'd spend the day telling her I love her and want her to be mine. I'm not a better man though. I barely even have enough emotions to care about my brother. I don't have enough to share with her too. I lose my temper often. I love my job too much to have time with anyone else. And my brother is a mess. I don't want to bring her into my troubles.

A loud snore escapes her.

I laugh. *So much for being an angel.*

And then the slow puddle of drool starts slipping from the corner of her mouth onto my chest. Usually, I would be disgusted. But there is nothing that Larkyn can do to make me turn up my nose at her.

I want to lie in bed with her all day, until I'm covered in drool and have heard every one of her cute adorable sounds she makes as she sleeps. But I need to deal with Sebastian. If Larkyn helped me realize anything, it's that I need to be tougher on Sebastian. And that ultimately, it's up to him, if he wants to change or not. As much as I threatened never to see him again yesterday, it's just not true.

Although, if he comes near Larkyn again or lays a hand on her, I'll punch him so hard he ends up in the hospital.

So with a heavy sigh, I carefully lift Larkyn's arms and legs off of me and slip out slowly, replacing my body with a pillow for her to wrap herself around. She smiles in her sleep, but otherwise doesn't stir.

It's early, but Larkyn usually gets up early, so I'm surprised she doesn't wake up. I grab my phone and type a quick message to her, so she knows I didn't abandon her. But then I hit delete.

If Larkyn wakes up without a message from me, that's a good thing. Last night, we shared too many emotions. Too many tears were shed together. Too much love was sparked between us. I have to keep my promise. That at the end of the year together, we will part as friends who spent a very enjoyable year together. Nothing more.

I slip out of the house without making a noise, jump into my McLaren, and take off toward Sebastian's apartment. I get to his door and pound on the door with my fist. He better fucking be here.

I don't hear anything at first, but my second round of pounding must have woken him up, because I hear loud stomps as he walks to the door. He opens it wearily, and I see the bruising that has formed around his eye. His eyes are still bloodshot from the alcohol. I take one whiff of his breath and know that he isn't hungover. He's drunk. At least he didn't drive anywhere. I took away all his cars and made sure to freeze his account for any payments larger than a thousand dollars, so he can't buy a new one.

I storm into his apartment and make myself comfortable on his couch. I need to calm the hell down if I'm going to survive this without killing him.

Sebastian takes his time walking over to a chair opposite me, stumbling into a seat before he picks up a beer and starts drinking from it.

I sigh. I see the pain in his eyes. Our father fucked him up. He emotionally and physically abused us both, then left us with no one to love. I was able to use that anger and funnel it into my businesses. But Sebastian, he's sensitive. He turned to drugs and alcohol, and now, there is nothing left of him.

"Let me help you," I say, keeping my voice calm.

Sebastian chuckles. "You can't help me. I ran a woman off the road. I almost killed her. And now the two of you are married or fucking or whatever the hell you are doing."

I take a deep breath, trying not to judge him. He's a good person. He just needs help. And I have no idea how to help him.

I rub the back of my head and look around his apartment, which is in desperate need of cleaning. Empty beer and whiskey bottles scatter the floor and tables. I can smell the rotting pizza in the kitchen from here. And I'm sure if I look closely, I'll notice ants, or possibly even mice, at home in his disaster of an apartment. Usually, I would call a cleaning service to help him. But I'm not going to this time. This time, he has to want to get better. I can't stay here and watch him slowly kill himself, but I can't keep fixing all of his problems, or he'll never get better.

"You need to go to rehab. Stop using alcohol and drugs as a way to crush your feelings; then you can figure out what you are doing."

He laughs. "Yea, because you are the model of healthy relationships."

I narrow my eyes, not understanding. "I have a great life. I work hard. I have great friends. I have an awesome brother when he's sober. I'm married to a beautiful woman. What more could I need?"

He shakes his head as he drinks the rest of the beer in the bottle that I want to rip from his hands.

"You are fake married. You may have friends, but you've never let a woman in. You won't because you're afraid if you really love someone, you might eventually turn into dad and treat her like crap. You're afraid you will drive away or hurt a woman, just like our father did to our mother.

"Just because you don't use drugs and alcohol doesn't mean that you are any better than me. You may seem to have your life together from the outside, but you still have no idea how to have a healthy relationship."

Every word he speaks is true. I don't know how to have a healthy relationship, especially with a woman. And I don't want one. I'm perfectly happy on my own.

I get up from the couch. I can't keep having this conversation with him.

"I want my business, Kade."

I glare at him. Hating that that's all I am to him.

"No."

He returns my glare as he stands up. Although, he's not that intimidating when he can barely stand upright.

"You don't have a choice. Father's will says that when I graduate from college, I am to be allowed to have one of the businesses."

My hands ball into fists next to my side, but I keep my composure and don't hit him again. If I do, I'm afraid it would do some serious damage. It might make me feel better, but it won't do anything to make Sebastian change his life.

"When you get sober, I'll give you one of the businesses."

I walk past him, ignoring him.

"That's not fair. Maybe having a responsibility, like having a company to run, would make me sober."

He looks at me, and my heart cools a little. He's just a lost boy that wants better, but isn't willing to do the work to help himself.

"You can't use a company as a reason to get sober. People rely on you to keep the company running. If you fuck it up, you'll be hurting other people. Whereas if you drink alone here, you'll just be hurting yourself."

"Why not? You do."

I stop in my tracks. Anger floods through my body until I'm trembling.

"I didn't come here to talk about me. I'm not the one with the problem. I came here to talk about you. Get your shit together."

A corner of his lip turns up.

"I'll have my lawyer talk to your lawyer about which company you will be passing onto me."

I grunt as I storm out of his apartment. He's not getting any of the businesses I've worked hard to grow until he proves to me that he takes his responsibilities seriously and is sober. I don't care if I have to spend all my time and energy fighting him in court, proving he isn't well enough to take over any of my businesses.

He's not tearing apart anything I've built. I came here wanting to get close to my brother again so that we could run the King empire together, but now I want nothing more than to go back LA and forget this town.

———

I OPEN the door to my bedroom, but Larkyn isn't there. It's after eight in the morning. *What did I expect?*

I walk down to her bedroom and knock on her door, but hear nothing.

I sigh. I'm going to need a drink soon to get through the day. I should make a couple calls to my lawyer first and maybe go for a run or something to get rid of my frustration. I head to my office. I open the double doors and slam them shut behind me.

Larkyn jumps as she sits on the couch in the corner of my office.

I cock my head to the side, as I slip my hand into my pockets, looking at her.

Her big eyes look surprised to see me home.

"Sorry, I didn't mean to intrude. Your office has the best light in the morning."

I walk over and sit down on the edge of the couch while she stays curled up in the corner with a book in her lap.

"It's okay. I'm glad you're here."

She smiles at me with sadness in her eyes.

"You went to see Sebastian."

I nod.

"It didn't go well, did it?"

"No, it didn't. I don't know how to get him help. He won't listen to me about going to rehab, and now he's demanding he gets one of the businesses that are owed to him."

She bites her lip as she puts down her book and scoots closer to me in her short skirt and tank top. She almost never wears skirts, so I don't know why she's wearing one today, but all I want to do is lift the skirt up and fuck away my feelings.

She places her hand on top of my hand.

"You were planning on giving him part of the bar business?"

"Yes. It's my favorite business, and I thought he would enjoy running it with me. We could split the bars in half or run them jointly. Or I'd be willing to give up that part, if it made him happy."

"And now?"

"Now, I don't want to give him any part of any of the businesses until he shows me he's responsible enough to take them over."

She strokes my hand with her thumb. And I feel it all the way to my groin. *Damn, I want her.*

My phone buzzes in my pocket. I pull it out, glancing at the name across the screen.

"My lawyer. I need to take this," I say.

"I'll go," she says, reaching for her book.

"Stay, you being close may help me keep my temper."

She licks her lip, and I almost consider not answering and fucking her. But if my lawyer is calling this early, it means Sebastian already contacted his lawyer.

"Yes," I answer.

"Sebastian's lawyer called."

"I was expecting that."

"Good, then you know that you have to give him one of the businesses. You don't have a choice. It doesn't matter if he is sober or not. Especially since you helped bury his most recent transgressions. You have no proof that he is sober or not. And if you do have proof, he'll end up in jail."

I run my hands through my hair. "Then what do you suggest."

"Give him the bars. They are the riskiest and least lucrative part of the business. And he won't have to do much, the managers at each bar basically run it themselves."

"Fuck, I can't give him the bars." I just fucking can't. They are my heart and soul. I could give the bars to him if he were sober. If he took this seriously, but not in his current state. I can't watch him destroy something I love.

I glance over at Larkyn who gets off the couch and wraps her arms around me as I stand in front of my desk. I start thinking through the financials of the other businesses, trying to figure out one that would hurt the King empire less or that he could run without even showing up, but I can't come up with any solution. The bars are the best solution.

"Give him the bars," I say, begrudgingly. Feeling my heart shatter, as I force each word out.

"Wait," Larkyn says suddenly.

I frown.

"Tell him you'll call him back in five," Larkyn says, looking at me with a big smile.

"Let me think about it for a few minutes, and I'll call you back."

I hang up and look at Larkyn as I cock my head to the side. "What?"

She sits down at my desk, flipping through my papers, like she knows exactly what she's doing.

"How often do you come into my office?" I ask.

She blushes. "Most mornings when I'm not teaching a class."

"And how often do you snoop?" I ask, as I sit on the edge of the desk with my arms folded and a scowl on my face.

She winces. "Just a couple of times. I find your business models and financials interesting."

I raise an eyebrow. "No one, but my accountant, finds this kind of stuff interesting."

She shrugs and grins when she holds up the paper she was looking for. She starts skimming the paper with her eyes.

"Here," she holds the paper up to me, which I realize is my father's will.

"I've read my father's will before."

She nods. "Of course, but did you read the part about the business that is to be given to Sebastian when he graduates from college? You are required to give him a main part of the business or any part that Sebastian chooses."

"Uh-huh, got that part."

She shakes her head. "You need to find something that Sebastian loves. Buy the business no matter how small, and then give him that."

I smile weakly, if Sebastian wasn't so far gone, her plan might work. But I don't think Sebastian cares about anything other than where his next drink is coming from and hurting me.

"The whiskey line makes you a lot of money. Your hotel line makes you more. And your bars, although they don't make you a lot of money, you are in love with them. If you give him any one of the businesses, he'll be filing for bankruptcy in a year. But maybe, if you give him something he's passionate about, he'll be more serious about it. Or at least if he fails, it will be on his own and not destroy you or your father's legacy."

I lean down and kiss her on the lips. "Thank you."

She rakes her teeth over her bottom lip as she leans back in the chair. "I'm more than a pretty face, you know."

I nod. "You definitely are. So why don't you have a real job?"

She shakes her head, her smile immediately dropping off her face like it never existed at all. "I don't want to talk about it."

"You bad at interviews or something? Because I can tell you if you are, I'd hire you in a second. I have trouble getting my own people to read shit like this. And you did it for fun, and actually understood everything."

She rolls her eyes. "I don't want a job."

"Why not? You need a job to make money. Work for me."

She gets up, storming across the room to distance herself from me.

"I had plenty of job offers when I graduated. I had one offer from Apple to run an entire project that would've paid me six figures."

My eyes pop open.

"I turned them down."

"Why?"

She fidgets with the hem of her skirt, pulling it up too high on her thigh.

"Because I didn't want to work for a corporation."

I smirk. "Because you want to freeload off a man like me

and live in a fantasy world where you can run and teach a few yoga classes and yet still live in a fancy house."

Her eyes bulge, her cheeks redden, and her lips tense along with her entire body. She looks like I just slapped her. I wouldn't be surprised if her face swells and forms a bruise even though I didn't physically touch her. She is beyond pissed. This is her kryptonite. She doesn't like it when I talk about needing a man to pay her bills.

"I can't believe I never saw how big of an ass you were before. I'm done running, at least in any professional sort of sense. And I teach yoga because I love it. And no, I don't plan on living off a man. Ever. I want more than just to teach yoga classes, but I want more than just sitting behind a desk making someone else's dream a reality."

I shake my head. "Yea, so that's why you agreed to our little arrangement. You get to live in the fancy house, while barely working. And you get a million dollars. What'd you do with the money, Larkyn?"

I pushed too far. I can see it in her eyes. Her ankle is still swollen, but she storms out so fast, you'd never know she was injured.

"I need you to go with me to a cocktail hour this weekend," I holler after her, hoping she will stop being pissed at me by this weekend.

"Go to hell!"

Yep, I pushed way too far this time. But it's for the best. Larkyn is better off without me.

15 LARKYN

KADE IS AN ASS.

He's worse than an ass. He's a cocky, arrogant, son of a bitch. He has no right to tell me I'm just living off him, when the only reason he is as rich as he is, is because of his father. Kade may have taken the businesses to the next level, but he got a whole lot of a head start from his father.

Just because I don't want to follow the same path and take money from my own father, doesn't mean I'm a spoiled princess. I thought he knew that about me, but apparently not.

I slip the diamond bracelet onto my wrist. I should tell Kade what I did with the money. It was his money first. He should know how I spent it. But not tonight. Tonight, I'm going to be the perfect date and act as if he doesn't affect me. Tonight, I'm going to show him just how committed I am to pulling my weight in this deal. That I'm my own person, and my life doesn't fall to pieces when he yells at me.

I step out into the hallway on my much too high heels and storm down the five feet to his bedroom. I should consider moving my stuff to the bedroom on the other side of the house. It's much bigger than my current room and gets more morning sun, which I love. I know the only reason he put me in this room was so I could be feet away from him.

I knock loudly on his bedroom door and wait. I push my hip to the side, posing as best as I know how. I don't smile, I don't want to appear fake, but I do moisten my lips and give little pout.

The door creeps open slowly until I see Kade standing in the doorway, looking as gorgeous as I've ever seen him. Dark grey pants with a white buttoned shirt, open at the top, with a dark grey jacket over it. He's shaved, but left just the right amount of stubble on his cheeks. And he's grinning like he knows just how much effort it took me to be standing in his doorway right now.

"I thought you weren't coming," he says, rolling his eyes up and down my body.

I can't focus when his eyes do that. So I wait until he's thoroughly checked out the slip on my dress that skirts the line between being slutty and sexy. Until his eyes finish their trail up the pink and grey dress.

"Finished?" I ask, swaying my hip out even more.

"Never."

I sigh. "I never said I wasn't coming. Just that you were an ass."

"That implied you weren't coming."

I roll my eyes and can't help but let my eyes linger behind him to his unmade bed. His bed is a million times better than my bed, maybe because Kade is always in it. I can't help that no matter how angry I am with Kade, I still want to end up in his bed tonight. *How pathetic does that make me?*

"I'm here. Are we going to this thing or not?"

"Absolutely."

He holds out his hand to me, but I turn and storm down the stairs to wait in the garage. We hop into his McLaren and take off to his event. And some-fucking-how, my hand finds its way into his. Honestly, I'm fucking screwed, because even when I hate him, I want him.

———

"WHAT IS THIS EVENT?" I ask, as we step into his bar. I never even asked where the event was, but I'm glad it's here. We both feel comfortable in his bar.

"Don't be mad."

I raise an eyebrow. "What the hell did you bring me to?"

He looks straight ahead, with a panicked look on his face. Our fingers are still interconnected, and I can feel a coldness shoot through his body.

I turn to see what he's looking at. Anastasia. Her fiancé. And my fucking family.

"Care to explain?"

He swallows and takes a deep breath, like that's going to save him.

"Anastasia booked her engagement party here."

"That doesn't mean that we have to be here!"

"She invited me as well. And unfortunately, I can't turn down an invitation to go to my wife's sister's engagement party. It wouldn't represent my kind-hearted appearance I've worked so hard to build."

"You mean your jerk, bastard, slutty reputation. The one that I married you to try to fix?"

He smirks. "Behave or don't. I don't care. I just got an

excuse to have my wife get all dressed up and go to an event with me. No matter how boring."

"You so owe me for this."

He wiggles his eyebrows. "And how will I ever repay you?"

His hand slides down the back of my dress, stopping on my ass.

I blush. *Damn him.* He's going to get me naked in one of the bathroom stalls most likely. *Ugh, why did I have to fake marry such a good-looking man?*

He brings his hand back up to a more appropriate spot in the middle of my back and guides me forward.

"You came. I didn't think the Kings had time for our measly little family anymore," Anastasia says, wrapping her arms around her fiancé. He doesn't speak; he just stands stoically. He's more of an accessory for Anastasia than a person.

"Of course, I wouldn't miss my sister's engagement party."

Anastasia holds out her ring to me. "What do you think? Is it too big?"

I want to say yes. It's far too big. And the only reason she has an updated version, twice the size of mine, is to compete with me.

"It looks great."

I take Kade's hand and excuse us toward the bar.

"I need drinks. Lots and lots of drinks, if I'm going to survive the night," I say, as we stand at the bar waiting for Axel to serve us.

Kade grins and motions for Axel.

"What can I get you, boss?"

Kade frowns. "Don't call me boss."

"We want two shots of tequila, and then I want a whiskey."

Kade eyes me out of the corner of his eye. "The same," he says to Axel. "Whiskey? Really?" he asks me.

I nod. "I need something strong to get through tonight. I don't care what it tastes like."

Axel returns quickly with our drinks, even though there is a long line formed around the bar of people that were here first.

"Thanks." I grab the first shot and down it, then snatch the second out of Kade's hand and drink his too.

Kade chuckles. "You better not get too drunk tonight. I wouldn't want to take advantage of you tonight," he whispers into my ear.

"You are absolutely going to take advantage of me tonight. I need something positive in my life tonight."

He laughs again, and I fall in love. I swear. All it takes now is a laugh, a smile, a look from him, and it's as if I've developed amnesia. I can't remember the bad, only the good.

"So what's the plan for tonight?" I ask.

"You stay by my side all night," Kade says, nodding toward a group of women that are eyeing him as if they are going to eat him up.

I smile. "Of course."

"We will stay long enough for your family to realize we are still happily in love, and then I'm going to fuck you in the back of my car. And then again in the foyer of my house. Then my bedroom. And anywhere else I can think of."

I choke a little on my whiskey.

Kade grins as he slowly sips his own.

I don't care he dragged me to my evil sister's engagement party. He probably did it to piss me off, but it's not working. Something about his charming smile makes it hard to stay too mad at him.

His phone buzzes, and he pulls it out without checking the number first.

"Hello, Sebastian," he says, with a hint of distaste in his voice.

I bite my lip to keep from smiling, because I know exactly what this call is about.

I can hear part of Sebastian's conversation as I lean against Kade's chest. But Kade doesn't speak. I look up, and the shocked expression tells me he can't.

I laugh and take the phone from Kade. He lets go of it easily.

"Hey, Sebastian. Kade has gone into a little bit of shock. Don't worry, I'm here with him. But know he loves you and is very happy for you." I end the call.

Kade stills, even more, if it's possible.

"Kade?"

"Sebastian is going to rehab."

I nod.

"He said you called him yesterday."

I nod.

"He said you were the one that convinced him."

I nod.

"Um... How is that? I mean...How?"

I smile. "I think Sebastian just needed to hear that he was forgiven. That what happened wasn't his fault. And then when he is done with rehab, he can choose any path he wants."

"I...uh...thank you."

"You're welcome."

"You're incredible."

His lips touch mine, telling me just how incredible I am.

His tongue sweeps into my mouth, and he might as well be sweeping me off my feet right now, that's how good the kiss is.

He tucks my hair behind my ear as he breaks the kiss. His lips tighten like he wants to say more but can't.

And I feel uneasy. I'm completely flushed, and I need a minute apart to cool down if I don't seriously want him to fuck me in the bathroom.

"Excuse me a moment. I need to use the ladies room."

I step out from his clutches and race to the bathroom. When I get there, I splash water on my face, not caring if it messes up my makeup. The water doesn't help, because I have butterflies dancing in my stomach all the way up to my chest.

I don't know what's real and what's pretend anymore. I don't know if that feeling deep in my gut is because I love him or hate him. I don't know if I wear the ring on my finger because I'm supposed to or if because I want this to be real.

I don't know anything anymore. All I know is that in a few minutes I have to step back out of this bathroom and pretend like nothing's changed. But I know deep in my heart, the second he thanked me for helping his brother made me want to spend the rest of my life loving him. Even if Kade doesn't always deserve it.

I dry off my hands, and then I walk back out to the party. Anastasia hasn't made any speeches, danced under a spotlight, or had all the attention on her in any way yet. So I expect when I walk back out that it will be about time for her to capture everyone's attention.

What I don't expect is for her lips to be pressed against my husband's.

I storm across the dance floor, not caring who I take out on my path. My heels clank against the floor so loudly I'm sure everyone can hear me. I glare at Anastasia even though I'm still twenty feet away. I've never hated her so much in my life. I don't know what she is thinking, kissing Kade. I know she is used to getting her way. But this is taking things too far. She can't just kiss Kade and expect he will fall madly in love with her, divorce me, and marry her. That's insane to think that. But I don't know any other reason she would have for kissing my husband than to torment me.

I get closer, and I start running. Planning on tearing the bitch from his lips and pulling her by the hair until I can throw her out with the trash.

Kade finally wiggles out of her grasp. And he looks pissed. Eyes dark, lips stern, and cheeks red.

"Get the fuck out of my bar!" Kade screams.

Anastasia folds her arms and raises an eyebrow. "Excuse me? I paid to be here. Not to mention, I'm your sister-in-law. You can't just kick my guests and me out."

Kade senses me and looks up. He struts over to me and holds me tight against his body.

"You are no sister-in-law. You aren't even a sister. You are a piece of trash that needs to leave now. Stop trying to manipulate your sister and me."

The entire crowd in the room has fallen silent. All eyes are on us. But I no longer care what any of them think. I'm just happy to have Kade hold me in his arms and defend me against my supposed family.

"You don't get to kiss me and get away with it. I want you out of my bar and out of our lives until you can apologize."

Anastasia's eyes panic when he mentions the kiss. And then she looks to me like I might save her.

"Out," I say, with the same fire in my voice as Kade.

Anastasia pouts before looking around the room at all

the prying eyes. It only takes her a moment to decide it might be best if she walks away. Her fiancé comes out of the bathroom, and several people point outside, telling him to follow Anastasia out.

"This is unacceptable, Larkyn," my father says to me sternly.

"Get the fuck out, Father," I say. I've had enough. I'm tired of being mistreated by my family. I'm tired of them thinking they are better than me. I'm tired of being told I'm wasting my life. I no longer care about any of it.

"Out, everyone, now," Kade's voice booms.

Axel and the other employees get to work shoeing everyone out the door. While I stay tucked in Kade's arm.

"I'm sorry," we both say simultaneously to each other as the crowd starts to file out.

I smile.

"I shouldn't have even engaged with Anastasia. I knew she was trouble and only wanted me for one thing. I should have been prepared for her kiss."

I shake my head. "I shouldn't have ever left you alone. I knew better. And you did warn me not to leave you alone."

He kisses me gently on the lips. "Don't ever leave me again."

His words sound so sincere, but I know they aren't. Time is ticking away. Less than nine months remain until our time is up.

"You okay, Larkyn? I'll swear Anastasia was the one that instigated the kiss and Kade was just an honest bystander who broke the kiss the second he could," Axel says.

I bite my lip with a smile. "You don't have to worry about defending Kade's honor," I tease.

Axel smiles. "Good. Anything I can get you? Need a stiff drink after that?"

I look up at Kade with dreamy eyes. There is only one thing I want right now to make me feel better.

"No, um...we are good," I say, stumbling over my words.

Axel looks from me to Kade and takes a hint. "I'm sending the staff home. The party didn't last long, so there isn't much to clean up. I'll have tomorrow's shift clean everything up before we open."

I swallow, my mouth dry as I stare up at Kade. He's handsome, and loving, and kind, and everything I've ever wanted in a husband. And he's my husband. Too bad this isn't real.

Kade watches Axel walk out of the bar, out of the corner of his eye. And then he grabs my ass, pulling me flush against his body as his lips crash into mine. We aren't going to make it home. We aren't going to make it anywhere. We need each other far too much after the emotional chemistry we have felt all evening.

Between me saving Sebastian, and him protecting me, we both owe each other a lot.

And we are about to make good on paying each other back.

I jump up, and he catches me as my legs wrap around his body. Our lips stay locked together in a dance that moves faster and faster, showing our true desperation.

"I can't wait. I have to have you—"

His lips cut me off.

And he drops me into one of the couches sitting around a low table, near one of the bars, as his body crashes on top of mine.

I grab his pants fumbling with the button until I can finally jerk his pants down.

I don't wait for him to remove my underwear, I push them down myself as his hand slides up my ass.

"Someone's impatient."

I tug on his bottom lip with my mouth, punishing him for stopping to do something as silly as talking.

He grins against my lips. "I don't know how I ever survived without you."

"Shut up and fuck me."

That makes him chuckle.

He slides his hand between my legs, finding the sweet spot that only he knows where it is.

I moan as his fingers move over my body, igniting me and making me want him to be his forever.

Our eyes meet as his cock nestles in between my legs.

He opens his mouth, and I'm afraid of what he might say. We both feel vulnerable right now. We both just showed we care about each other more than we have ever let on. And that scares the crap out of me, because if he doesn't tell me he loves me, or at least what he is feeling is real, then I might explode in pain.

He hesitates, and it can't be good, so I kiss him, and it takes away whatever he was about to say away.

His cock pushes inside me, and I arch my back, begging his body to go deeper inside mine. Our eyes meet together, as bodies entwine. Our eyes stay open, together, as we both come.

We stay together a long time, neither of us speaking or moving. Kade finally pulls out of me, does his pants up, and then helps me up from the booth.

We both have so many things to say, but neither of us says them. Instead, we walk to Kade's car, and he drives us home with nothing but the radio to keep us company.

I try not to let my mind race, but it's difficult. All I can think about is how much I care about him. How much I want this to be real.

I rest my head against the window and close my eyes. If I sleep, maybe in the morning I'll have a different perspective on my life. Instead of the heartache, I feel at the thought of losing Kade.

The car eventually stops as I doze off to sleep. I feel myself being lifted into Kade's arms, but my eyes are far too heavy to open. My head flops against his chest, and my breathing is heavy as Kade carries me inside and into my bed. He doesn't bother undressing me; he pulls the covers over me as he sits on the edge of the bed.

I want him to climb in the bed next to me, but I know that would only make things worse. Our feelings are clouded enough.

Kade leans forward and kisses me softly on the lips. A perfect kiss to take with me as I fall asleep.

"I love you Larkyn," Kade whispers, thinking I'm asleep. But I hear his words, or I dream them.

"But you can never be mine."

16 KADE

HOW THE FUCK did I fall in love with Larkyn?

I have no idea, but it's a problem. I'm breaking the one promise she swore she needed above everything else. I fell in love, and now I'm going to hurt her. And I'm pretty sure she is in love with me, or at least has feelings toward me too.

I need to talk to Larkyn. We need a new plan if we are going to survive these next several months without hurting each other. I just have no idea what the plan is.

"I made dinner for you," Larkyn says, coming into my office and putting her arms around my chest like it's the most natural thing to do.

Dinner would be the perfect time to talk to her. Tell her we need more boundaries. That she needs to start treating me like an ass too, because I'm falling far too hard for her.

"Sounds great, what did you make?"

She grins far too wickedly. "Your favorite."

I raise an eyebrow as I follow Larkyn, who is basically dancing with giddy excitement, as she runs back to the kitchen.

I follow her at a slower pace, enjoying watching her show from behind.

And then I smell it. Garlic bread and marinara sauce.

I grin. "You remembered."

She laughs, as she stirs the big pot and begins scooping out food into a bowl.

I can't contain myself. I wrap my arms around her as I take a bite over her shoulder.

It tastes horrible.

I make a scrunched up face, unable to hide my disgust. Maybe this is just what we need. A playful, relaxed night where we have to order take out and realize we aren't perfect for each other.

She pouts.

"Your *first time* making spaghetti?" I ask.

She nods, biting her lip.

Her eyes turn to slits of lust. "But I have a way to make it taste better."

I raise an eyebrow. "By throwing it in the trash and starting over?"

She giggles. "No, you're lucky I like you or I might consider that too mean."

"It's not mean. It's the truth. That is the worst thing I've ever tasted. You somehow managed to burn it, and the seasoning is all off. Did you use cumin? You know that is usually used in Mexican dishes, not Italian?"

Larkyn turns, holding a spoonful of the sauce up to my lips. "Oh come on, it isn't that bad. Try it again."

I close my lips tightly. "Nope, I'm not eating another bite."

She cocks her head to the side as her hips pop out. She stands taller until her breasts are fully popping out of the low cut sundress she's wearing. She has a twinkle in her eye that I know means I should run. Far, far away, because whatever she is about to do is trouble.

Instead, I stand intrigued like the idiot I am.

She turns the spoon over, and red marinara sauce drips down onto her breasts.

"Oops," she says, smiling slyly.

Fuck.

My mouth falls open, and an instinct that is all man and testosterone takes over my brain. I forget about how bad the sauce is. I forget about talking to her. All I can think about is licking the marinara sauce off her tits.

I'm to her body in second. My tongue runs down her neck and over her breasts until I'm licking every drop of the sauce clean from her tits. More drips down between her breasts that I can't reach.

I rip the dress open, as she stumbles backward into the counter. She grabs another scoopful of sauce and rubs it over her chest and stomach.

It shouldn't turn me on, but it does. Anything she does turns me on. I remember back to the conversation when I told her I would love a woman to be covered in marinara sauce. It was a fantasy. One that I never thought to act upon. But seeing her covered in red sauce makes me do a weird cross between laughing and wanting.

She looks hot and ridiculous at the same time. And I've never wanted a woman more. Not because she looks sexy, but because she planned this. She made me spaghetti so that she could seduce me with a wild fantasy I once told her.

I set her up on the counter and spread her legs apart. Her hands run through my hair, rubbing red sauce all over my head until it's dripping down my face. I move to wipe it off with the back of my hand, but she leans down and slowly rubs her tongue up from my chin, over my lips, then nose.

I growl. "When did you become so sexy?"

She blushes. "I've always been sexy."

I rake my teeth over my bottom lip. She's right about that.

She grabs the hem of my shirt and lifts it off, making sure she covers my chest with the marinara. She reaches for my pants, but I really don't want sauce all over my cock. So I use my left hand, that is still relatively clean, to lower my pants and release my cock.

She reaches down to stroke me. It takes every drop of strength I have to push her hand away. I want her hand on me. Desperately. But I don't want to be covered in red, sticky sauce.

So instead, I push into her opening as I grab her ass and surrender my body to her. I've never felt this way before whenever I've had sex with a woman. I don't just want to bring her pleasure. I want to make her mine in every way possible. I want to rule her world and her mind. I want her to never think about anything other than me.

She smiles at me, then arches her back, and I lose her pretty eyes to the pleasure pulsing through her body.

"Look at me, beautiful."

She slowly tilts her head back to me and forces her eyes open.

"Gorgeous."

She blushes and stays with me as I feel us both building.

I try to tell her everything with my body. That I love her.

That I want more than a fake marriage.

But I'm terrified of hurting her.

I don't know how to protect her from the damage I'm

capable of. Because for as much crap as I give Sebastian, I've been there. I've never abused alcohol and drugs, but I've buried myself in women or work. No matter what damage it caused other people.

I don't know how to treat Larkyn as a partner. I don't know how to truly let her into my life.

I come inside her as she screams her own orgasm. And as much as I desperately tried to tell her how I'm feeling, she doesn't have a clue at my inner turmoil.

Larkyn grins mischievously, as she fluffs my hair that is drenched in the disgusting sauce.

"I told you I could make it taste better," she says, with a wink.

I laugh and lift her off the counter. "Sorry, but it tasted disgusting the entire time. You have officially squashed any more dreams of getting to lick marinara sauce of your body."

She grabs a handful of the sauce from the pot next to me and flings it at me.

I duck, and the sauce scatters on the floor around me, but mostly misses me.

I grab her, lifting her up before she has a chance to attack me with the gross liquid again.

She squeals and flails in my arms as I carry her to the shower in her bedroom.

"Why aren't we showering in yours? Your shower is bigger."

I chuckle. I put her down on her feet in the shower. "Because I didn't want to drip gross marinara sauce in my bedroom or shower."

She scoops some off her chest and rubs it into my face while I grimace.

"Don't lie, you love it."

I turn the water on and watch her squeal as the cold

water comes down on top of her. I love the sound. Just like I love everything about her.

I should break up with her. It would be the right thing to do. Release her from our contract. Set her up in a nice home and let her live her life in peace.

But my heart has fallen into the deepest part of love. I can't stop it. I can't control it. And I know that this is going to end horribly. Because I'm less than perfect. I'm a human with plenty of flaws. And one of those flaws is going to come crashing into our lives and screw us both, until I'm left with nothing, but heartache and pain.

I love her. But I'm not enough for her. She's going to realize it as soon as I fuck up. I've managed to hang on this long, maybe I can stop myself from fucking up for years, so that I can at least have some more time with her.

Or maybe, I should break up with her, and spare her the heartbreak before she falls in love with me.

"SO WHAT SHOULD we celebrate with? Wine? Champagne? Whiskey? Margaritas?" Serena asks, as I sit across from her at our favorite lunch spot.

"And what exactly are we celebrating?" I lean back in my chair. We are definitely celebrating something, Serena just doesn't know what it is yet.

"Spending time with each other, for one. It's been four months since you got married and we've barely hung out. So we are celebrating us getting back together again."

I laugh. "Fine, order whatever alcohol you want."

"Margs it is then."

I smile sweetly at her. "How are things going with work?"

"I'm doing amazing. I've already been promoted and got a huge raise. I've fixed their ridiculous filing system. My employers have realized they can't live without me."

I chuckle. "Sounds like you have thoroughly charmed them."

She nods. "Enough about my boring job though. How are Kade and you doing?"

I can't look her in the eye as I fidget with the napkin in my lap. "We are good."

She squints trying to look for something. "We're good. That's all I get? How's the sex?"

I laugh nervously. "Amazing. Not that I have a lot to compare to—"

Serena snickers.

"But I have no complaints in the sex department."

"So what's the problem?"

"I don't have a problem."

She stares at me, deadpanned. "You have a problem." She turns to the waiter. "Two margaritas please."

I sigh. "It isn't real."

Serena rolls her eyes. "I've seen the way that boy looks at you; it's real."

I tense. I know she's right. That we have feelings toward each other. But neither of us have acted on them in four months. It's been over a month since Kade said he loved me when he thought I was asleep. He's not mentioned anything like it since. Not one word. And my own heart has flipped back and forth so many times; I'm not sure what I feel anymore. One second I love him, the next I hate him.

"What about the job or life search as you call it? Have you figured out what you want to do with your life?"

I lick my lips, trying to find the words to tell her what I've been hiding for two weeks now. I need to tell someone, and she's that someone. But as soon as the words leave my mouth, I have to actually act on the words. I sure as hell don't have time to look for a meaningful job when I'm holding in a secret that will change my life forever.

"No, I haven't found anything."

Serena frowns. But the frown doesn't last as our server

places two large margaritas in front of both of us. She lifts her glass up, and I do the same.

"To many more sleepless nights, as we both get to fuck two of the hottest and most endowed guys in town," Serena says.

I clink my glass with hers and then set mine down.

She studies me a moment. Looking me up and down. "Oh my god!" she squeals.

"Shh," I say, not wanting her to blurt out her next words too loudly.

"You're pregnant," she whisper-yells, as she leans across the table. At least she attempted to be quiet.

I nod.

"Does Kade know? Was it planned?"

I shake my head.

"Were you using protection?"

"The pill."

"When are you going to tell Kade?"

I shrug.

Serena laughs and gets up from the table and comes over to hug me. "At least I get to drink two margaritas for lunch."

I smile and lean into her chest. I don't know what I'm going to do. I'm pregnant. With Kade King's child. We are fake married. We aren't even in a real relationship. But we are having a baby. And I have no idea how Kade is going to react when I tell him.

I'VE BEEN AVOIDING Kade all day.

I've gone to the grocery store multiple times to pick up things I forgot on previous trips.

I went to the post office to get stamps, not that I have anything to mail.

I filled my car up with gas and drove through two separate car washes.

I thought somehow doing those mindless tasks would bring me some clarity of mind and help me figure out how to tell my fake husband we are pregnant. *For real.*

How do I tell a man, who thought this was nothing more than a fake arrangement, that we are now bonded together for life, whether we want to be or not?

How do I even start that conversation?

I don't have the answers as I slowly walk into his house. I close the door carefully, hoping if he doesn't hear me enter, I can stall having the conversation for a little longer.

Stop being a chicken.

I clear my throat. "Kade?" I holler as I walk into the kitchen. It's around dinner time, but he's not in the kitchen. I hear voices down the hallway where his office is. Maybe he has a client back there, or Axel is over discussing things as they usually do?

I start walking down the hallway toward his office. I need to tell him I'm home and ask if we can chat later. Otherwise, I'll lose my nerve again and won't talk to him until tomorrow or the next day or the next.

My hand raises over his closed door to knock. He never closes the door, so it's strange it's closed now. My hand stops in midair.

"This is your child, Kade," a woman's voice says.

I still. *Did Kade knock up more women than just me?*

Kade laughs, like it's the funniest thing in the world. "The child isn't mine, Harlow. I can do the math. The last time we had sex was in January. This child is too young to be mine."

"I'm filing to sue you for child support. Or you can give me five million to make this all go away. It will be far less than what I get when I win my case."

"No. I want a paternity test, because there is no way that child is mine." A pause. And I feel tears threatening my eyes.

"And even if the child is mine. So what? I'll provide child support. I'll make sure the child has the money he's owed. But that's it. You aren't getting a penny of my money. I'll make sure every penny I give you goes to the child. And even then, your child won't inherit anything. You won't mean anything to me. I never wanted a child. Certainly not yours."

Tears pour out of my eyes like lava. They burn more and more, the heavier they flow out. I don't care if he knocked up Harlow. I don't care if he has a child other than the baby growing inside me. All I can focus on is five little words. *I never wanted a child.*

I force my legs to run away to my bedroom where I let all the tears fall. And in their place, the anger comes.

All the times that Kade has been a jerk to me flood my head. And most of all, the fact that even though he might feel love for me, he's never acted on those feelings. He doesn't want me.

He doesn't want our baby.

I won't listen to him cause me pain. But I can't stay here either. I want out.

I head to the bathroom, dry my eyes, and pinch my cheeks, trying to look like I haven't spent the last ten minutes crying, and then I storm toward the kitchen where I can hear Kade cooking.

"Hey, dinner will be ready in ten minutes," Kade says.

I can't wait ten minutes.

I pull the heavy ring off my finger and place it on the counter.

Kade raises an eyebrow. "Something wrong with the ring?"

"No, something is wrong with whatever this is that we are doing."

He stops stirring the delicious smelling Asian dish he is making and faces me.

"I'm sorry Larkyn, but I don't understand, and I've had a shitty day, so I'd love it if you could speak plain English and get whatever fight we are about to have over with."

"I'll make this easy for you then. I want out of our contract. I'm done being fake married to you."

He blinks rapidly, and then narrows his eyes at me, as he cockily crosses his arms. "You can't be serious."

"I am."

"Why?"

"Because I'm tired. This isn't what I thought it would be."

He cocks his head to one side. "And what did you think would happen?"

"I thought that you would buy me jewelry every other week, take me to fancy parties, and go on nice vacations with me. I thought I would get to enjoy more of the perks of being your wife," I say, lying through my teeth. I don't care about any of those things, but I know that money is sensitive with Kade. It's the main thing we've fought over. What I did with his money. And after Harlow tried to blackmail him for money, I have no doubt he is very sensitive about the subject now.

He narrows his eyes like he's looking through to my soul. "What would it take for you to stay?"

I wasn't expecting him to talk so calmly about this or to ask me that question, but I know my answer immediately.

"I want five million dollars," I say, lying. All I want is his heart. I want him to love his future child the way that I do. But that's asking too much.

He doesn't even flinch, and I think he might say fine. He'll do it. Maybe if he's willing to pay me five million dollars when he just denied it to Harlow, that means I'm special to him. Instead, he stands stoically looking at me while he reads me like an open book.

"What did you do with the money I gave you?"

I can feel my stomach clenching as he speaks. I'm about to be sick. I can't stay here much longer without upchucking. And yet I can't force myself to leave because I know these are our last moments together.

"I bought the most expensive house I could afford with it."

His eyes drop in disappointment. "Then, I'll have my lawyer draw up the terms to release you from my contract."

He walks toward me looking me dead in the eyes. I can't move. All I can do is smell his familiar smell of a deep cologne. I take in the last flicker of his dark eyes, and the curve of his lips as he frowns.

"You owe me nothing. And I owe you nothing. I'll put into the media that the divorce was amicable. And then we are done." When he says the word done, he turns and walks back to his pot, stirring it like we didn't just have the soul-crushing conversation we just had.

Contrastingly, it takes everything in my body to turn and walk to my bedroom before my stomach empties into the toilet. I don't know where I'm moving or what I'm doing with my life. I don't know if, in a few years, I'm going to regret ever agreeing to fake marry Kade or if I'm going to appreciate it because I love our child so much. I can't think beyond this moment. Because in this moment, I'm pregnant, and alone.

18 KADE

"WHAT ARE you still doing here? I can handle this, go home," Axel says next to me, as I clean the bar for the fifth time.

"I know you can handle it, but I want tonight to go perfectly," I say, ignoring him as I continue to clean. I don't add that it has been three months since I've seen Larkyn, and I'm losing my damn mind. I can't think, I can't sleep, the only time I can even pretend to function well is when I'm at work, and that's only because there is something for me to focus on to keep my mind off things.

"Go home. You hired me to be the manager. Now let me do my job and go home. I've dealt with plenty of corporate events before. I can handle making sure the bar is clean." Axel snatches the rag out of my hand.

I glare at him.

Axel looks back at me sadly, like I'm a stray puppy without a home or something.

"I'm fine. Don't look at me that way."

He shakes his head. "You are anything but fine."

"Yeah, you're an idiot," Sebastian says, taking a seat at the bar across from me.

"Should you be in the bar after just getting finished with your treatment program?" I ask.

"Bars aren't a trigger for me."

I frown. "What are your triggers then?"

"Anger, resentment, feeling betrayed, losing focus, and parties. No party, no need to drink."

"There is a party here tonight. You can't stay."

"I don't plan on staying."

I roll my eyes. "You just plan on calling me an idiot again and then leaving?'

He shrugs. "Something like that."

Ugh, I need a drink, but I'm not drinking in front of Sebastian. He's been sober for two months now. I won't be the reason he screws that up. Which is also why I'm not letting him hang out in the bar.

"Well, tell me how much of an idiot I am so that we can get on with our lives."

Sebastian gives a smug smile to Axel, who leans against the bar to join our conversation.

"You're an idiot because you broke up with Larkyn; filed for divorce even. You need to call her," Sebastian says.

"No, she made her decision. She doesn't want to be with me."

"Just call her," Sebastian says.

"No, that's enough. If you just came here to talk about Larkyn, I'm done," I say, giving Sebastian a warning glance. He may be my brother, and he may be getting his life together, but I've slugged him before, I'll do it again if he pisses me off.

Sebastian nods slowly, his head bobbing several times.

"Fair enough. Then, I guess I don't have anything else to say." He turns toward Axel. "Can you get me a club soda?"

Axel tightens his lips and then makes a club soda for Sebastian and himself. He slides the drink to Sebastian.

"Have you heard from Larkyn lately? I know she used to love this bar," Sebastian says, staring at Axel.

"I know what you are doing, and it's not going to work," I say, annoyed.

"No, she hasn't come in lately. How has she been?" Axel asks, both men ignoring me completely.

"She's doing well. Really well, actually," Sebastian answers.

"That's awesome. Where has she been working? Is she still at the yoga studio?" Axel asks.

Sebastian grins. "No, actually, Larkyn and I started a business together. A non-profit. It's a healing center meant to help people that are struggling. It provides them a place to stay, people to talk to, and connects them with the treatment they may need. Larkyn's been running it with me. She occasionally helps teach a yoga or fitness class, but she mainly runs it as my business partner."

I listen to Sebastian. I can't help it. But then I already knew what she was doing because as much as I should leave her alone, I can't help but stalk her online.

"Is she seeing anyone?" Axel asks, his eyes cutting to me.

I growl.

Both men smirk. "Not that I'm aware of, but then again, we are only business partners. She doesn't tell me everything," Sebastian says.

"Okay, you've had your fun. Get out," I say, annoyed with both my best friend and brother.

Sebastian and Axel laugh. Sebastian stands. "Fine, fine. I'm going."

Sebastian's phone buzzes, and he pulls it out of his pocket. "Hey, Larkyn." He smirks at me as he answers the phone.

My blood is boiling, but I also really want to hear her voice on the other side of the phone, so much that I lean over the bar so that if an opportunity presents itself, I can snatch the phone out of Sebastion's hands.

"Wait Larkyn, slow down. What do you mean he's out?"

My heart stops. I don't know what's happening, but I hate the way Sebastian's voice just hiked up several octaves higher.

"No, don't leave your house. You have a security system, and he shouldn't be able to find where you live. I'll be there in five. Lock all the doors, and arm the security system until I get there. And try to relax. He's not going to come straight for you after getting out of prison. I'll call my lawyer on the way over and see what's happening with his case and if he'll end up back in prison soon," Sebastian says.

"Nathan got released on bail?" I ask, unable to contain my anger in my voice.

Sebastian nods.

"I have to go," I say, as I hop over the bar and start running toward my car. I hear Sebastian behind me, but don't wait for him.

I run and jump into my McLaren in one motion, enter the address I know she's lives at into my phone, and then take off as the directions appear on my phone. I've never driven by Larkyn's house, but I had my lawyer find her new address for emergencies like this or for when I couldn't stand to be apart from her for another second.

If Nathan so much as lays a hand on her, I'll kill him. Larkyn has been through enough. He doesn't get to touch her. Ever. She's mine.

He was supposed to stay locked up this time. I reported that he was dealing cocaine again, even though, I didn't have evidence. Just a hunch. My statement was enough for his parole officer to do a random search. Turns out he was dealing again. He was supposed to be locked up again for years.

It takes me five minutes to get to the address. I park my car, but don't even bother to turn off the ignition. I need to get to her. Last time Nathan was released, he went straight for her. I won't let him hurt her again.

I run up the driveway and take in the cute modest house in front of me. It definitely isn't a million dollar house, but I wasn't expecting it to be. It looks exactly like Larkyn. Independent, adorable, and perfect.

I knock on the door, pounding loudly with everything I have while I beg her to answer. She can hate me, but I need to see that she is alright.

The door creeps open the tiniest crack so that I can only see her head as she peers around the door.

"What are you doing here?" she asks.

"What are you doing answering the door when there is a known criminal on the loose?"

She frowns. "I saw you on my security camera Sebastian helped me install." She nods toward the corner of her porch. I see the tiny camera staring right at me.

"Let me in. I want to stay with you until Nathan goes back to prison."

She shakes her head. "I don't think that is a good idea. Sebastian will be here any minute to help. And I've already spoken with the police. There is nothing we can do until his next trial date later this month. He's out on bail."

"Please, let me stay. I won't be able to breathe if I don't know you are safe," I say, looking deep into her eyes and I can see her caving. She wants me here as much as I want to be here.

I put my hand on the door, gently pushing it open, hoping that once it's open, she will invite me in.

We both stop breathing as the door swings open, and I get a full view of her. She's beautiful, but there is something different about her I can't place. She's happier than she was with me, maybe that's it. I can't keep my eyes off her body. I scan her body up and down. Over her tight jeans and stomach that is protruding the tiniest bit over her jeans.

I narrow my eyes and look again. There's a bump. Not a huge bump, but definitely a bump. One that is very noticeable on her usually smooth, rock hard stomach.

My eyes meet Larkyn's, and her eyes glisten with moisture. She's about to cry.

"You're pregnant?" I ask.

She nods, swallowing hard.

"It's mine, isn't it?"

She nods.

"Larkyn, I'm so sorry, I was an ass." A smile creeps up on my face as I realize I'm going to be a dad, and the woman I love is going to be the mother. This is my chance to change things, to make things right.

"No," she says, as I move toward her.

I stop. "Please let me fix this. We are having a baby together. Let me fix things."

Her lip trembles, but she doesn't back down. "There is no together. No us. I'm having a baby, and you can be in this baby's life or not. I'm not looking for money, or child support, or inheritance. I would love for my child to have a father, so if you would like to be in my baby's life, then we can get our lawyers together to discuss a custody arrangement. Otherwise, I don't want to see you again."

"Larkyn, please let me explain—"

Her eyes aren't looking at me anymore; they are looking past me.

I glance behind me and see Sebastian standing on the foot of the porch.

"I can go if you two need more time to talk. I'll do whatever you want me to do, Larkyn," Sebastian says, ignoring me.

"Come in," she says, and Sebastian steps inside her home. A man she once hated for almost running her over; she now welcomes in so easily. But me, a man who loves her, she views as a betrayer. I still don't know what sparked her to fight with me the night she left, but it was clear she wanted out, that's why she said what she did.

"Please," I beg, as I bend down on one knee, like that will somehow convince her.

"I'm sorry," she says, closing the door.

And then I'm alone on her porch.

So instead, I say what I need to say to her, to her front door, and hope she's listening. "It was all fake. The reason we aren't together. The fighting. All fake. I love you, Larkyn. I was an ass because that's what you needed. I would do anything for you, and I thought I was doing the right thing by pushing us away from each other. But I was wrong. We belong together.

"I know you are upset about how I kept pressuring you about what you did with the money. But I've known all along what you did with the money. I've always known. You didn't use it to buy this house. And I love you more for it."

No answer. Not that I was expecting one. I let my hand rest against the door for a second, needing to be as close to her as possible.

And then I walk over to the bench on her porch and sit down on it. I'm not moving from this spot until I see Larkyn again. She needs to know I'm here for her and our baby no matter what. And that starts with actions, then maybe she'll listen to my words.

"KADE IS SLEEPING on your front porch," Sebastian says, peering through my blinds.

"So?"

Sebastian drops the blind he had lifted up and walks over to the small white couch to sit next to me. I found this couch at a thrift store, and I love it.

"So, don't you think you should give him another chance?"

"No."

"You gave me another chance and look how that turned out," he says, wiggling his eyebrows to try to make me laugh. It's not going to work.

I sip my tea. "No."

Sebastian sighs. "You have to talk to him at some point. He is your baby's father."

"That's what I have lawyers for." I tuck my feet underneath me as I rest my teacup on my leg.

Sebastian reaches out and touches my leg lovingly. "I'm meeting with a few people this morning to work on the building construction. I can cancel if you want me to stay here."

"No, I'm fine. Besides, I have my trusty guard outside."

Sebastian gives me a weak smile. "You two had better have talked to each other and made up by the time I return."

"Don't count on it," I say, returning to my tea.

Sebastian gets up and walks out my front door. I peak around to see if Kade will try to sneak in before Sebastian has a chance to lock it, but I see no signs of Kade. *Maybe he went home?*

I finish my tea, and it's mid-morning, but I'm already exhausted. I don't have any meetings today, but I do have a lot of emails to go through. First, I need a nap; then I'll get to the emails.

I grab the grey throw draped over the back of the couch and pull it over me, curling up on the couch. I should be thinking about how I'm going to get the courage to talk to Kade, but all I can focus on right now is sleep.

————

I FEEL his hot breath on my neck.

I smile.

Kade.

I don't care that he snuck into my house. Or that he's breathing over me. Or that he woke me up from a much-needed nap. I'm just happy he's fighting to be in my life.

I open my eyes. And jump to my feet when I see the eyes staring back at me. They don't belong to Kade. These eyes are far too evil.

"Nathan," I say, stepping backward trying to reach for my phone on the coffee table behind me. But when I reach the coffee table, I feel nothing.

Nathan smirks. "Looking for this?" he asks, holding the phone up.

I take a deep breath and stare at the door behind me. Kade will hear. I need to talk loudly, and he'll call the police. But when I glance out the window and see it's dark outside, my confidence fades. *How did I sleep the entire day away? Where is Sebastian? And did Kade manage to sleep on my front porch for another night?*

"What do you want, Nathan?" I ask, trying to think of what to do next to keep Nathan occupied.

"I'm here for you, of course."

I nod. Trying to stay calm as I grasp my belly. *I won't let him hurt you*, I think.

"You don't want to do this, Nathan. You are free. You should go live your life."

He glares at me. "I'm out on bail. I'll be going back as soon as you testify against me. You're nothing but a fucking liar."

I swallow. "I won't testify to anything. I can't. What happened between us was a long time ago."

Nathan steps closer to me, and I freeze, just like before. I can't save myself. I'm not strong enough.

He reaches out to grab my arm, and finally, I snap awake.

"No," I cry loudly, not this time. I swat his hand away and run toward the front door.

I grab the doorknob and pull, but the door is locked with three different locks. *Why didn't I think about how to make a quick escape?*

I turn the first lock.

Then, the second.

I reach for the third, high up on the door, when Nathan's hands squeeze my neck.

I cry out as he pulls me away from the door.

"Help!" I scream, finally finding my voice. "Someone help me!"

Glass breaks in the window over the porch, and Kade's body comes barreling through. He doesn't stop until he reaches us, knocking us both to the ground as he goes after Nathan. I roll away from the two men as I watch Kade punch Nathan in the face over and over. Blood spews everywhere. And Kade easily wins the fight.

"Call 911," Kade says, pulling his phone from his pocket and holding down Nathan.

I call, and within minutes we hear the police sirens. Kade gets a few more punches in before the police arrive. They handcuff Nathan and take our statements. They all insist I go to the hospital, but I don't want to spend the day in the hospital, so instead, I have a medic check me out, and after promising to make a doctor appointment for tomorrow, just in case, we are left alone.

"You're safe now," Kade says, stroking my face. "I guess I should go too." He glances toward my front door.

"No."

His face lights up, but the sternness of my face dissipates any happiness on his. This isn't going to be an easy conversation.

"I love you, Larkyn," Kade says.

I bite my lip. I've been waiting months to hear him say those words to me and mean them.

I nod, because I can't force my lips to say them back. Not until I hear more. Because if I admit I love him, and this doesn't work out between us, my heart will break worse than when Nathan attacked.

"I know you set up a foundation to help people. That's what the money went to. I know that money is now being used to start the non-profit with Sebastian to help people heal from whatever pain they are dealing with."

I nod. I'm sure Sebastian eventually told him the truth.

"What you don't know is I've always known. From the first day you set up an account to use the money for charity, I knew. My lawyer tracked the money and found out for me. You can talk to him if you want. He'd never lie for me. It's a problem really." He smiles and sticks his hands in his pockets as his adorable dimples form on his cheeks.

"If you knew, then why did you constantly ask me? Why did you make me feel like a gold-digger for taking the money?"

"Because you asked me to."

"Huh?"

"Because you asked me to be an ass so you wouldn't fall in love with me. So I was an ass. I knew that was a sensitive topic for both of us that I could easily play up and piss you off with. That's all it ever was."

I think back to all the times he screwed with me, and I know he's telling the truth. I asked him to make me hate him so that I wouldn't fall in love. And every time we got close to falling in love, he did something that made me mad.

"I'm not leaving you. Or our baby. Ever."

I shake my head. His words aren't enough. "I heard you with Harlow."

"I told her the truth. There is no way her baby is mine."

I nod. "I know. I heard you say you never want children. I don't want to trap you with a baby. This will never work."

Kade's eyes narrow, and he walks out of my living room. Then out the front door. While I stand frozen.

I don't know what he's doing or if he's coming back. And I hate that I don't know if he's coming back.

A few minutes later he returns with papers in his hand. He thrusts them into mine.

"Read this paragraph," Kade says, pointing to the third paragraph.

I start reading the page that I realize is the contract I signed a few months ago when we agreed to fake marry. But I don't believe what I'm reading.

"You added this page. This wasn't here on the contract I signed."

He frowns. "This paragraph was included the whole time. You just didn't read the contract very well."

I shake my head. "I read the contract front to back ten times before I signed it. I know better than to sign a contract like that without reading it first."

"Go get your copy of the contract."

I sigh. This is pointless, but I walk to my makeshift office in the corner of my dining room. I dig through the stack of papers until I find the contract, and then I bring it back and thrust it into Kade's hands. He flips through the pages, but can't find the one he's looking for.

He flips to the third page, studies the paper for a second and then begins pulling at the corner. Two pages are stuck together. And when he pulls them apart, and I see the paragraph. Tears fall from my face, most likely forming puddles on the floor near my feet.

"You wanted a baby this whole time. It's encouraged in the contract, but ultimately up to me if I want to pursue or not. You think I'm the perfect woman to have a baby with, and you want an heir because you are probably never going to get married for love. And you would love a child with a woman you care about, to love, to be your heir, and keep other women from trying to get knocked up so their child would become your heir," I say, paraphrasing all the important parts of the contract.

He nods.

"You want this baby?" I ask.

"As much as I want to spend the rest of my life loving you."

He wipes the tears from my eyes. "Will you have me? Let me try to make up for all the horrible things I've done to you. Love you and this baby and—"

I don't let him finish. My lips land on his in the most passionate kiss. "I've always been yours, from our first kiss, to the first time we had sex. Even when you pissed me off, it didn't make me love you less. It just made me mad."

"Then, you'll let me love you for real, forever?"

"You can love me for as long as you can stand me," I say, still sobbing as our bodies collide together.

He kisses me over and over.

"I'll never get enough of you, beautiful. I loved you even when you wouldn't let me. I just didn't know how to convince you to love me through your fear."

"Now you don't have to, because I'll never be afraid again as long as I have you."

"When do I get that five million bonus in the contract for having your baby?" I tease, not believing he thought I would ever be after his money.

He smirks. "I think I owe you half of my money, my businesses, and my heart. We may have been fake married in our hearts, but on paper, our marriage is very real."

I smile. "I like real."

EPILOGUE

KADE

"YOU ARE NOT PROPOSING to me again," Larkyn says, brushing past me to rearrange the flowers at the entrance of the sanctuary that she and my brother created together. I'm a little jealous, actually, that he gets to work with her every day. They've created something incredible, and today is the grand opening.

I smirk. "How did you know I'm planning on proposing again?"

She flashes me a glare, but all I can do is laugh, because her heart isn't in it and it turns more into a half smile, half grimace.

"Because I know you. You won't leave my side, you bought me a new dress to wear today, and you bought enough flowers to fill my entire house."

"Our house," I say, referring to her home that we moved into together. I wasn't sure I would like the smaller, more modest home. But I love that there are fewer places for her to escape to and hide away from me. And I like that it gives us a fresh start.

"And can't I just do something nice for you?" I ask.

"No, you are up to something."

Larkyn grabs the vase of flowers and moves them from the right side of the front desk to the left side.

I wrap my arms around her stomach from behind and feel her relax in my arms. I love that I simply have to touch her and she melts.

"Everything is going to be perfect. Now stop fussing, and kiss me," I say into her ear.

Her head leans into me as I speak in her ear. I turn her head toward me as I kiss her, not able to let go of her stomach, where our baby is due any day now. She turns her body toward me to deepen the kiss and her arms wrap around my waist. I grin against her lips when her hands grab my ass, then slide toward the front of my slacks shocking me. I might get to fuck her in her office.

"Ah, hah! What is this?" she asks, pulling a tiny box out of my pocket.

I shrug. "I don't remember putting that in there."

She glances down at my mother's ring that hasn't left her finger since the night we told each other we loved each other and wanted to make this real. I would never replace that ring with another.

"You didn't buy me another ring, did you?" she asks, exacerbated with the idea of me buying her more jewelry.

I grin. "Open it and find out."

She eyes me and the box carefully. And then opens it. She smiles and shakes her head, as she pulls the tiny hand-made heart out with a note attached that says: *You're mine forever.*

She looks at me unsteadily as her eyes grow bigger, and I know, if I do this right, she'll cry, and I'll get to see her gorgeous tear-streamed face filled with love.

"I didn't want to propose. I know you don't want me to.

And I don't either, but I wanted something special to cement our new relationship before this baby comes," I say, placing my hand on her stomach.

Her lip trembles.

"We don't need a redo. Everything I've ever felt for you was real. The pretending, the marriage, the love. All of it real. The only thing fake was when I treated you like crap."

"I don't want a redo either."

"We don't have to get married again, or go through a proposal or any of that. I just wanted you to know that I will spend the rest of my life finding ways to tell you and show you how much I love you, forever."

She kisses me, and I forget about my speech or what I was planning next. I know I need to wrap this up soon so we can officially open her business to the public. But I need a few more stolen moments with her. As soon as her business is open, and we have this baby, I know my stolen moments with her will be few.

"I'll be yours forever, as long as you promise never to be an ass again."

I smirk. I love calling herself mine. I love it when she calls me her husband or her baby daddy or any of the words she uses to describe me too. She loves me. And I love her. I was afraid, for far too long, of screwing up and becoming my father, but the only thing I needed all this time was the right woman, one that I didn't want to screw up with.

"Can I be an ass twice a year?"

She raises an eyebrow at me.

"Never being an ass is too hard," I say.

She laughs, and I can't believe I'm lucky enough to get to listen to her laugh for the rest of my life.

"Fine, but you'll be sleeping on the couch any time you are a jerk. And you have to do cute things like making me handmade hearts to win me back after you fuck up. But no more pretending to be a jerk because you enjoy watching me squirm."

I smile; I never want to be fake with her ever again. "Deal."

The End

Thank you so much for reading! Sebastian has his own story to tell! Preorder Pretend We're Over Here!

I'm not looking for a date. I'm definitely not looking for a husband—just one night of passion. I'm in Vegas, after all. And what happens in Vegas stays in Vegas.

So how did I end up with a giant rock on that finger, you ask? Your guess is as good as mine.

Now I'm stuck fake married to the biggest self-centered jerk I've ever met. We agree to keep the charade going for six months to protect our pride and dignity. We have six months to convince everyone we aren't meant to be. Should be easy.

I'm sweet, kind, fun Millie.
He's cynical, self-absorbed, loner Sebastian.

We don't belong together. Convincing everyone we're married is the easy part. Convincing everyone we're over— that's proving more difficult. Convincing myself that we're over is proving hardest yet.

I just have to remember that it was all pretend from the

start. We were never together. Pretending we're over is just going back to my life before. But what if I don't want to keep pretending?

Pretend We're Over is a standalone fake marriage spinoff featuring Sebastian.

Coming July 21st 2020
Preorder Pretend We're Over Here!

ALSO BY ELLA MILES

SINFUL TRUTHS:

Sinful Truth #1

Twisted Vow #2

Reckless Fall #3

Tangled Promise #4

Fallen Love #5

Broken Anchor #6

TRUTH OR LIES:

Taken by Lies #1

Betrayed by Truths #2

Trapped by Lies #3

Stolen by Truths #4

Possessed by Lies #5

Consumed by Truths #6

DIRTY SERIES:

Dirty Beginning

Dirty Obsession

Dirty Addiction

Dirty Revenge

Dirty: The Complete Series

ALIGNED SERIES:

Aligned: Volume 1 (Free Series Starter)

Aligned: Volume 2

Aligned: Volume 3

Aligned: Volume 4

Aligned: The Complete Series Boxset

UNFORGIVABLE SERIES:

Heart of a Thief

Heart of a Liar

Heart of a Prick

Unforgivable: The Complete Series Boxset

MAYBE, DEFINITELY SERIES:

Maybe Yes

Maybe Never

Maybe Always

Definitely Yes

Definitely No

Definitely Forever

STANDALONES:

Pretend I'm Yours
Finding Perfect
Savage Love
Too Much
Not Sorry

ABOUT THE AUTHOR

Ella Miles writes steamy romance, including everything from dark suspense romance that will leave you on the edge of your seat to contemporary romance that will leave you laughing out loud or crying. Most importantly, she wants you to feel everything her characters feel as you read.

Ella is currently living her own happily ever after near the Rocky Mountains with her high school sweetheart husband. Her heart is also taken by her goofy five year old black lab who is scared of everything, including her own shadow.

Ella is a USA Today Bestselling Author & Top 50 Bestselling Author.

Stalk Ella at:
www.ellamiles.com
ella@ellamiles.com